UNION'S END

BOOK FOUR OF THE STAR SCAVENGER SERIES

G J OGDEN

Cover design by Grady Earls
Editing by S L Ogden

www.ogdenmedia.net

THE STAR SCAVENGER SERIES

READ THE OTHER BOOKS IN THE SERIES:

- Guardian Outcast
- Orion Rises
- Goliath Emerges
- Union's End
- The Last Revocater

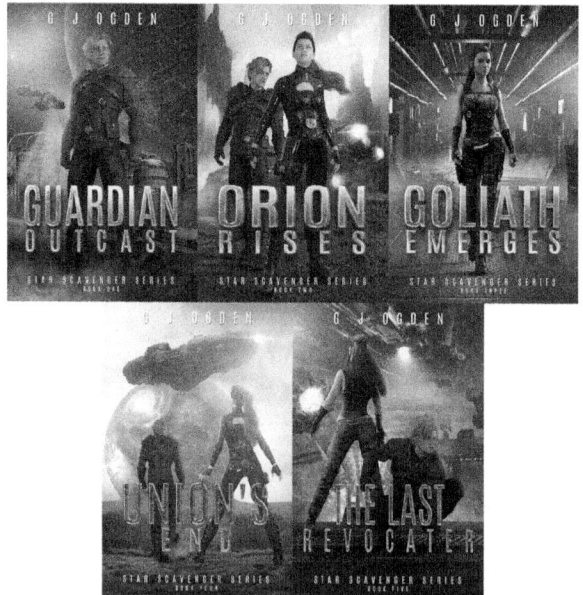

ACKNOWLEDGMENTS

Thanks to Sarah for her work assessing and editing this novel, and to those who subscribed to my newsletters and provided such valuable feedback.

And thanks, as always, to anyone who is reading this. It means a lot. If you enjoyed it, please help by leaving a review on Amazon and Goodreads to let other potential readers know what you think!

If you'd like updates on future novels by G J Ogden, please consider subscribing to the mailing list. Your details will be used to notify subscribers about upcoming books from this author, in addition to a hand-selected mix of book offers and giveaways from similar SFF authors.

http://subscribe.ogdenmedia.net

PROLOGUE

The Telescope had at one time provided the Corporeals with a limitless window on the galaxy. Along with the creation of the crystals and portals, it was one of their greatest and proudest technological achievements. Using the portals like lenses, the Telescope could refract its signal from one part of the galaxy to another. Never losing integrity, the signal would travel from portal to portal, on and on, until the object of the Corporeals' interest came into sharp focus.

The Telescope provided the Corporeals with visibility of every inhabited world they had seeded. For thousands of years, they watched and waited for the first of these worlds to reach a stage of cultural and technological evolution that finally meant they could reveal themselves. For eons the Corporeals had been alone in the galaxy, but soon they would have companions to share it with. With little more of their own culture and knowledge left to expand, this had become what the Corporeals lived for. They craved new art, literature, songs and stories to share. They yearned for new conversations and new points of view, even for arguments. Anything to shake up the status quo.

They had been patient, wary not to reveal themselves to a species that was much less advanced. The Corporeals did not want to appear to their celestial neighbors as gods, to be feared and revered. Instead, they sought the company of equals. However, Goliath had other ideas.

When the great ship had begun its rampage of destruction and extermination through the galaxy, the Telescope took on a new purpose. Instead of passively watching the many inhabited worlds, like a bird watcher in a hide, it now aggressively sought out Goliath. The great ship, with its vast intellect, had jumped unpredictably from system to system, to avoid being ambushed. To a casual observer, its movements would have seemed chaotic, even mad. Yet Goliath knew precisely what it was doing. And it knew precisely where it was going.

Incapable of predicting Goliath's next target, the Corporeals were unable to concentrate their Revocater armada into a single fighting force. Goliath knew that it was not strong enough to defeat them all. Instead, with no predictable pattern to its attacks, the Corporeals were forced to station a Revocater at each of their seed worlds.

The Corporeals believed that these solitary guardians possessed the might to thwart Goliath's rampage. However, they had underestimated the great ship's cunning. A single Revocater was easily controlled. It was exactly the situation that Goliath had sought to engineer.

The only warning a Revocater would get of an attack would come from the Telescope. If the Corporeals could spot Goliath's arrival soon enough, the Revocater stationed in the system could intercept it. The intention was that their colossal warships would destroy Goliath, before its presence was ever discovered by the worlds it sought to destroy. The hope was that the seed populations would remain blissfully ignorant of the titanic battles that would be waged to protect them. However, Goliath was too ingenious, too devious, and too ruthless. It invaded the cores of the Revocater pilots and twisted their programming to serve its own will. Then it used the Revocaters to exterminate the civilizations they had been sent to protect. The Corporeals could do nothing but watch the slaughter from the Telescope orbiting above their home world, powerless to intervene. By the time another Revocater could be sent as backup, Goliath would have already resumed its erratic ballet of jumps.

The Telescope had seen horrors unimaginable to most sentient beings, but had endured them willingly. It had to keep its eye focused on Goliath, so that it would warn the Revocaters in time. Yet one by one it watched them fall, until only one last Revocater remained. Then, when all hope was lost, Goliath was conquered, and banished to the galactic core. A single seed world remained, but the last Revocater was also lost. Or so the Telescope thought.

For millennia, the Telescope had secretly watched Goliath, ever fearful that the great ship might discover a way to return. Then the unthinkable happened – Goliath emerged from its prison of isolation and began a course back to System 5118208. The moment it had dreaded for eons was here. Yet in the midst of darkness there was still hope. The last Revocater was alive, and it was coming home.

CHAPTER 1

Cutler Wendell and Logan Griff walked back into the cockpit of the FS-31. They had just returned from restoring the patrol craft's drive systems, after the transit through the new portal from Sapphire Alpha had knocked out the main reactor. Both were wiping grease and oil from their hands, using worn and dirty rags that had been used for that purpose dozens of times before.

Tory Bellona had already begun to steadily accelerate away from the newly-opened portal, towards the closest planet in the system. However, even from tens of thousands of kilometers away, it was immediately apparent that this system was different to all the other portal worlds that had been discovered.

"The closest planet to the portal is a gas giant," said Tory, as Cutler slid into the second seat. "I'm picking up low levels of Shaak radiation in orbit around it." Then she looked over to Cutler, appearing slightly perplexed, "You'll need to run a more detailed scan."

Griff hustled over and stood between the two seats, grabbing the headrest of each. "What does that mean?" he asked, gripping the padded fabric tightly. "Are you saying the wreck crashed into the damn gas giant?" The prospect that they'd managed to stumble upon the only portal world ever discovered that didn't have a wreck to scavenge was making him nauseous. If there was no wreck then the planet was worthless to the RGF. His grip tightened further, as he considered all the different ways that Superintendent Wash could blame and punish him for such a titanic failure. "Is there a wreck or not?" Griff snapped, unable to contain the pressure that was building up inside him, like a geyser ready to erupt.

"Why don't you just shut up and wait?" Tory hit back. She was angling her body away from Griff, clearly uncomfortable with his current proximity to her.

Cutler didn't answer, and instead continued to quietly analyze the scan results. The wait for the computer to process the data was becoming unbearable. Then, finally, Cutler spoke up.

"The Shaak radiation is definitely coming from objects orbiting the gas giant," he began. "The material analysis would suggest that they are fragments of an alien hulk."

"Damn it!" snapped Griff, releasing the headrests and punching them in frustration. Tory glowered at him, and Griff quickly moved his hands to his sides, though they were still balled into fists. "Of all the portal worlds out there, we had to find the only damn one without an intact wreck to scavenge."

Tory laughed, and Griff glared down at her, though he was careful not to aim his clenched fists in the mercenary's direction. "What's so funny? No wreck means no pay day," he growled, "and, in case you've forgotten, the Council are after us." Then he remembered Tory's background and laughed, realizing she was ironically in less danger than he was. "But I guess a former indentured thug like you will just be put straight back into service, right?"

"I'm never going back to the Council," said Tory, with a sudden, fierce determination. "I'll die before I let them take me again." Then she locked eyes with Griff, and added, "And I'll kill anyone that tries to double-cross me, or turn me in."

As insinuations went, Tory's was as obvious as the wiry black mustache on Griff's face. However, he held his tongue, conscious of the mercenary's fiery temper.

"This system may still have value," Cutler interrupted. He had continued working on the scan data, while Tory and Griff sparred.

"What do you mean?" asked Griff, springing beside Cutler's seat so he could see his monitors more clearly. Cutler's words had given him hope that something of their operation could be salvaged. At that moment, he'd take anything that might spare him from Wash's spiteful fury. "Is there another wreck?"

Cutler shook his head, "Not another wreck, but I am detecting structures on the largest of the gas giant's five moons."

Griff frowned as he looked at the information on Cutler's monitor. The scan data meant little to him, but to Griff's eyes, the long-range images certainly suggested the presence of cities on the surface. He smiled and stepped back, unfurling his fingers.

"We might have struck pay dirt after all," said Griff, plucking a cigarette out of the black packet in his shirt pocket.

Tory scoffed a laugh, "I don't think the auction houses pay much for alien rubble..."

Griff glared at Tory again, "Who gives a shit about broken alien ships?" he said, refusing to let Tory's pessimism sour his reinvigorated mood. "We have entire cities worth of relics to pick through." He laughed again and placed the cigarette in his mouth, before taking out his lighter. "Who knows; this could be the most valuable little planet in the entire galaxy!" Griff flicked open the lighter, but no sooner had the flame sparked into life than Tory spoke up.

"Light that thing in here, and I'll shove it down your throat, lit end first."

Griff glanced over to Cutler for support, but he didn't even acknowledge Tory's threat, and continued to stare at his screens. Their alliance had always been a fragile one, based on shared interests, but their relationship now seemed to be resting on a knife's edge.

Griff closed the lighter and plucked the cigarette from his mouth. "Okay..." he said, before reluctantly sliding the stick back into the packet. "Since you asked so nicely."

"Tory, I've sent you the co-ordinates for the moon," said Cutler, again acting as though he was oblivious to Griff and Tory's quarrelling. "I suggest we move quickly; we don't know how long we'll have before others arrive."

"Fine by me," said Tory, adjusting course for the moon. "The sooner we bag a good score, the sooner we can get rid of the bad smell in here."

Griff's blood was almost boiling over, but he bit his tongue again. Then Tory pushed the throttle forward, sending Griff staggering to the rear bulkhead. The force of the acceleration wasn't enough to make him fall, but he knew Tory had done it deliberately all the same.

"Oops, I'm sorry, did I forget to remind you to sit down and strap in?" said Tory, glancing back and grinning at Griff. "You might want to take a seat, Inspector. I'd hate for you to get hurt..."

Griff clambered away from the bulkhead, pulling himself forward using the side consoles like a handrail. He then dropped into his seat and fastened the harness. He was desperate to hit back at Tory, but he could no longer rely on Cutler to support him, or intervene. He had no doubt that Tory would love nothing more than to stick a knife in his throat. However, since Cutler's announcement that the Council would be hunting for them, he now worried that the mercenary might be having similar thoughts. When the Council boss, Werner, eventually caught up with them, someone would have to take the fall for Liberty having escaped New Providence. Griff's preferred choice was Tory Bellona; he'd love nothing more than to stitch her up, and teach her a lesson. However, he wasn't sure if Cutler had a similar plan in mind. And, despite the recent tension between Cutler and Tory, Griff wasn't yet convinced that Cutler wouldn't make him the fall-guy instead.

However, Griff also knew that none of that mattered until he had a big score under his belt. For now, he had to bide his time. As soon as the RGF controlled the new portal world, he'd go back to Superintendent Jane Wash and ask for her protection from the Council. It would cost him in credits, of that he had no doubt, but at least he'd be safe. Then he'd be in a stronger position to negotiate with Werner. However, while the Council hunted them, and until he had earned

Wash's trust and favor again, he still needed Cutler and Tory.

"Just get us to that moon," said Griff, relaxing back in the chair. He was desperate for a smoke, but he didn't want to risk that Tory's inventive threat had not been a bluff. "Cutler is right, other hunters will be racing each other to get here next. And it won't be long before the CET and MP make an appearance too."

An alarm sounded in the cockpit, and Griff could see a red light illuminate on Cutler's console. He sighed heavily, and called out to him, "What the hell is the matter now?"

Cutler seemed strangely uneasy, considering his normally unflappable demeaner. He was working frantically at his console, and again choosing to ignore Griff. This made him feel immediately on-edge. There wasn't much that managed to rattle Cutler Wendell.

"Do you see that?" asked Tory, frowning over towards Cutler.

"See what?" Griff called out. He hated being out of the loop; he was used to being in control, not only of the mission, but the ship too.

"I see it," replied Cutler. "Analyzing now…"

"What the hell do you see?!" Griff called out again.

Tory glowered back at him, "Will you shut up already? You're like a damn child, constantly asking 'are we there yet?'."

Cutler was the one to eventually answer Griff's question. He glanced back and met Griff's eyes. In them he saw something he very rarely saw from Cutler Wendell – fear.

"There is another ship or object on an intercept course," said Cutler.

"What other ship?" asked Griff, not following. It didn't seem possible that anyone else could have made it to the Sapphire-Alpha side of the portal yet. "Who is it? Another hunter? The CET, or MP?"

Cutler shook his head. "It isn't any of those. It isn't anything I've seen before." Then he hesitated, seemingly struggling to force the words out. "It appears to be... alien."

CHAPTER 2

Griff watched anxiously as Tory throttled back so that the FS-31 was no longer accelerating towards the oncoming alien vessel. She then pulsed the port thrusters, pushing them into a slightly different trajectory. The unidentified alien ship mirrored her maneuver exactly, and remained on a collision course.

"Whatever that thing is, it's tracking our movements," said Tory. Her tone was urgent, but not panicked. "If we stay on this course, it will smash right through us in a little over three minutes."

Cutler reached over to a secondary console and activated the FS-31's hidden weapon systems. He then pulled the targeting console in front of him and locked on to the alien vessel.

Griff frowned as the motorized whir of gears deploying the weapons rattled through the deck.

"What are you doing?" Griff called over to Cutler. "Surely, you don't intend to shoot at it?"

"I don't know what that thing is, and I don't care to find out," replied Cutler. "So yes, as soon as it is within range, I intend to destroy it."

Griff stroked his wiry mustache anxiously. He freely admitted to being more of a 'shoot first, ask questions later' personality, but usually he knew what he was shooting at. And firing at an unknown alien ship seemed like an incredibly risky gamble. Now, more than ever, he wished he was on his own patrol craft, and not at the mercy of Cutler's decisions. He knew as well as the others did how important it was to find a good score on the new moon. However, there was a universe of difference between tackling rival hunters and pompous CET and MP starship captains, and dealing with an unknown alien threat.

"We should turn around now," said Griff, choosing to be the voice of reason. "I've got a bad feeling about this. We should head back to the portal and wait for the RGF fleet to arrive."

"And lose our chance at a big score?" replied Cutler, in a condescending tone that instantly got Griff's back up. "I haven't come all this way to leave with nothing, Inspector. And if your RGF friends arrive on that moon before we do, you know full well that I will be cut out of the profits. That is not going to happen."

Griff was about to argue back, but Cutler turned away and addressed Tory instead. "Is it just flying directly at us?"

Tory nodded, "Other than matching any move I make, yes. Its course is arrow straight."

Cutler flicked a couple of switches on his weapons systems console. "Good, then it will just fly straight into our shells," he said.

"If this doesn't work, our window to withdraw will be gone," said Tory, again calmly but with measured urgency.

"It's not like you to back down, Tory," replied Cutler. From the subtle change in the tone of his voice, Griff thought this was bordering on an insult.

Tory glowered back at Cutler, "I'm not backing down," she said, clearly angered by Cutler's response. "I'm just letting you know that if you do this, we're committed. No going back."

Cutler didn't acknowledge Tory, and finished activating the weapons systems. Griff watched as the targeting reticule appeared overlaid on the cockpit glass. A blue triangle materialized, flashed and then remained solid. Griff glanced over at the monitor to the side of his seat, scanning the tactical information. The ship was small, roughly equivalent to a large taxi flyer or two-person shuttlecraft. While he was studying the monitor, Griff noticed a strange glow coming from below. He glanced down and saw that the window in the scendar device he'd stolen from Hudson's ship was glowing brightly again. *What the hell?* he asked himself, leaning over to get a better look. He was about to highlight the discovery to Cutler, but then he felt two solid thuds punch through the ship.

"Forward cannons fired," said Cutler. "Their trajectory looks good."

Griff frowned down at the scendar again, but then concentrated on the tactical overlay on the cockpit glass. Although he would have preferred to turn around and run, he was also eager to see the effect of Cutler's attack. If the alien ship was destroyed then all was well, other than him needing to suffer Tory's inevitable gloating.

"Impact in ten seconds..." said Cutler. No-one else spoke. Griff counted down in his head, then there was a brief flash of light ahead.

"Did you get it?" Griff blurted out, realizing he hadn't taken a breath the whole time he was counting.

Cutler again didn't respond. Griff's own sense of powerlessness, combined with Cutler's infuriating lack of communication, was driving him crazy. "Cutler, damn it, did you destroy the thing or not?!" he growled.

"No... the shells appear to have had no effect," replied Cutler, sounding anxious. Then he again turned to Tory, "Can you outrun it?" The question was asked timidly, because, like Griff, Cutler already knew the answer.

Tory shook her head, "Like I told you, it's too late for that now," the mercenary replied, severely. "If running was the plan, we should have turned back when it first appeared."

"Shit!" Cutler swore, in a rare display of emotion. It was yet another unusual reaction from the typically unflappable mercenary. "Turn around anyway. If we pull a high-g burn, it might give up its pursuit."

"It's too late, damn it!" snarled Tory, her own voice finally showing some signs of stress. "The burn would kill us. I told you if you stayed the course then we were committed. So, I say let's find out if this alien bastard wants to play chicken!" Tory locked in her course, and stared out ahead, her eyes wild.

"Tory, what are you doing?!" yelled Cutler, "Turn away, now, that is an order!"

"I'm done following your orders!" Tory hit back, refusing to alter course. "I'm not leaving this system with nothing, and I'm never going back to the Council! I'd rather die here. So, we're going to find out who breaks first."

Griff was speechless, but then the engines of the FS-31 suddenly cut out, and it spun one hundred and eighty degrees. The rapid and unexpected movement would have thrown Griff from his seat, had he not still been strapped in. He steadied himself against the console to his side and saw that

Cutler had overridden Tory's controls, and was now flying the ship himself.

Heart pounding in his chest, Griff checked his monitor again, and saw that the alien ship was still coming for them. They had less than a minute.

"Damn it, Cutler, we can't outrun it!" Tory snarled, hammering her fists onto the flight deck. "At least go down fighting, not running away like a coward!"

Cutler ignored her and continued frantically preparing to initiate a hard burn away from the alien ship. Griff's eyes flicked nervously from Tory to Cutler and back again. The female mercenary was incensed.

"To hell with all this," said Tory, unclipping her harness and darting across to the center of the console. She then grabbed the FS-31's ID fob and yanked it clear. Immediately, the ship's drive systems went offline; it was like switching off the ignition of a car.

"Tory!" yelled Cutler, trying to grab the fob back off her, but he was still strapped into his seat, and he merely flailed his arms at her helplessly.

Tory then walked up to Griff, and drew her revolver, "And to hell with you," she growled.

Griff stared at the weapon, immobilized by fear. Then he peered up into Tory's cold, resentful eyes, as the mercenary clicked back the hammer of the six-shooter and aimed the barrel at his head.

CHAPTER 3

Griff squirmed in his seat as Tory slid her finger onto the trigger of the six-shooter. However, with the harness still fastened tightly, he was trapped and helpless.

"Tory, come on, think about what you're doing!" Griff yelled at her, now fixing his eyes onto the barrel of the revolver.

"I know exactly what I'm doing," replied Tory, "It's something I should have done a long time ago. But, since we're all going to die now anyway, I'll be damned if some alien thing gets to be the one who takes you out."

There was the sound of another weapon being loaded. Griff glanced behind Tory to see that Cutler was aiming his pistol at Tory's back. He was still in his seat, but he'd swiveled it to face them.

"Tory, sit down," growled Cutler. "We still have a chance, but not if you put a hole in the hull!"

Tory glanced back at Cutler, and then at his pistol. "I'm going to put a hole in this asshole, not the ship. But shoot me if you want. I don't give a shit anymore."

With Tory's head turned, Griff saw his chance. With seconds to act, he unclipped his harness and threw himself at Tory, tackling her to the deck. There was a sudden, deafening crack as the revolver fired, and for a second, Griff thought he was hit. Then the console behind him erupted into sparks and flames, and alarms rang out inside the cockpit.

Griff clambered off the deck, with Tory still lying stunned beneath him. He grabbed the ID fob that had fallen out of Tory's hand when she fell, and staggered between the two main seats.

"Go, quickly!" Griff yelled, holding the ID fob to the initiator. The device snapped into place, and he heard the drive systems begin to cycle online. However, Cutler was just scowling down at the navigation scanner. "Cutler, what the hell are you waiting for?!" Griff cried again, shaking the mercenary's shoulders, "the drives are online. Go!"

Cutler brushed Griff's hands away angrily, "Wait... the alien vessel is no longer tracking us," he yelled back, before pulsing the thrusters to push them into a subtly different trajectory. "It now appears to be merely drifting towards us."

Griff peered down at the navigation scanner, and saw that Cutler was right. The alien vessel was no longer tracking their movements. "What did you do?" Griff asked, feeling the grip of terror relax its hold on him slightly.

Cutler shook his head, then leveled off the controls and throttled back. The alien ship continued on, making no further attempts to match their course. "I don't know. I did nothing, at least nothing I am aware of. But it appears that the danger is past."

"The danger is past?" repeated Griff, sounding incredulous. "We don't know that!"

"Control yourself, Inspector," Cutler hit back. His disdain was clear, just as it had been when Cutler had lost his cool on the alien station. Cutler then removed his harness and moved out in front of Tory. She had landed hard, but was now sitting up, back pressed against the bulkhead, looking at Cutler.

"Did you hear that, Tory?" said Cutler. He was aiming his pistol carefully at Tory's head, to avoid the protection offered by her armored jacket. "We're in the clear. So, everyone can relax."

Tory stood up slowly, with Cutler tracking her all the way. She glanced over at the navigation scanner on Cutler's console, which confirmed his statement, then met Cutler's eyes again. "I meant what I said, Cutler. I'm never going back to the Council. If I have to take you all down with me, I will, believe me."

"I believe you," replied Cutler. Then he turned his head fractionally towards Griff, and said, "Inspector Griff, please set us back on a course towards the moon. We have work to do."

Griff couldn't believe what he was hearing. After what had just happened, he had no intention of steering the ship back towards the moon. "Are you insane? There could be more of those things out there!" he said, looking back into the mercenary's eyes. However, Cutler had again placed a tight lid on his emotions, and all Griff saw was calm determination. Still, Cutler wasn't the one calling the shots, and it pissed him off that he again had to remind the mercenary of that fact.

"This is my mission, Cutler," Griff said, jabbing a nicotine-stained finger at him. "And I order you to head back through the portal! Let the RGF fleet check out this system first. We can always find another portal, and another wreck!"

Cutler's eyes narrowed fractionally, before he pointed back to the console next to Griff's seat. It was still crackling and smoldering gently, as a result of Tory's wayward shot. "I'm afraid that isn't going to be possible anymore, Inspector," Cutler added.

Griff frowned and looked back at the console. "Shit!" he cursed, while dropping down on his knees in front of the damaged device. Tory had put a hole directly through the glass window. "This thing is ruined," he said, digging out the fractured glass so hc could get a clearer look inside. Then he shook his head despairingly. "And the bullet has cracked the crystal in half too." His head fell forward. His temples were throbbing, and it felt like needles were being pushed into his eyeballs. Wash was going to kill him when she found out, he realized. However, one system under RGF control was still better than nothing. And maybe the RGF techs could repair the device. Maybe he could still salvage something from this mess.

"Ironically, perhaps the destruction of the device is what saved us," said Cutler.

"How do you figure that, genius?" snapped Griff, pulling himself up into the more comfortable pilot's seat, while still massaging his temples.

"The alien vessel broke off its pursuit the moment the device went offline. Perhaps it was drawn to it, like a moth to a flame."

Tory huffed a laugh, "So, what you're saying is that I just saved everyone's life?" Then she cocked her head towards Cutler. "Maybe you should be thanking me, rather than pointing that little pea shooter at my head?"

Cutler's expression remained serious, "Without that device, we can't open another portal," he continued, fixing Tory with an unblinking stare. "Which means that the moon out there is our only chance to score something worthwhile."

Griff shook his head again. "Our percentage of all claims from this system will dwarf anything we can grab before the RGF fleet arrives. We head back while we still can. That's an order!"

"I think we are all past the point of taking orders from you, Inspector," said Cutler. He was much calmer now, and his surly, monotone delivery had returned. "Our situation is bleak. And I cannot risk that your precious Superintendent Wash will renege on our agreement," Cutler went on, though he was still aiming the pistol at Tory. "And even if she honors the bargain, it could be months before those payments reach us. The Council will have found us all long before then."

Griff silently cursed. From Cutler's perspective, what he'd said was true. He couldn't be sure that Wash would honor her agreement, even to him. However, the difference with Cutler and Tory was that they weren't RGF, and he was. The RGF failed at many things, but taking care of their own was not one of them. He needed to get back to the portal, and back to safety. Even without a score from the new portal world, his best chance of survival was to get back to Wash, and spin it as best he could. Yet he also knew that Cutler was laying out these facts not for his benefit, but for Tory's. Despite being held at gunpoint, if Tory agreed to follow Cutler, he'd be outnumbered and outvoted.

"So, what's it to be, Tory?" asked Cutler, after an anxious silence. "Will you join with me for one last hunt? Then we shall both be rich enough to part ways, amicably. Or shall we go back and face the Council with nothing?"

Tory folded her arms. She was still wild, but she no longer looked like a hungry wolf that was being dragged away from its kill. "Okay, so we go to the moon and take what we can," said Tory. Then she bent down and picked up her antique Colt Frontier Six-Shooter. Griff held his breath again as she grasped the weapon, but let it out slowly as the mercenary slid it back into her holster. "But after this, you and me are done. Understood?"

"Understood," replied Cutler, flatly. He then also holstered his weapon, before turning to Griff. "And what about you, Inspector Griff? Will you join the hunt, or would you prefer to continue barking pointless orders and wasting our time?"

Griff shook his head, "I think you're both crazy. But it doesn't look like I have a choice."

"No, you don't," replied Cutler, before dropping into the second seat and unlocking the controls.

Tory paced up in front of Griff, who was still in the pilot's seat, and stared down at him. Griff felt his heart start to pound in his chest again. His eyes flicked nervously to the revolver on Tory's belt. However, Tory just raised her eyebrows, and gestured towards the third seat. "Are you going to get the hell out of my way, or am I going to have to drag you out of my chair?"

CHAPTER 4

Morphus came back online. For a few moments, as its core reinitiated, it was disorientated and unsure of where it was. Then its memories flooded in, repopulating its circuits like water filling a dried-up river. It was back at the Corporeals' home world, docked at one of the few orbital repair docks that had survived Goliath's assault.

Morphus ran a quick diagnostic and discovered that the damage to its systems had been repaired. Its power reserves were depleted, and it would take time to recharge them, but otherwise it was functioning normally. However, it also felt strange, and somehow different to how it remembered. Then it realized why; it was no longer in its humanoid form, but stored inside its processing capsule, shapeless and indistinct. Despite this being its default form, and despite the entirely inorganic nature of its construction, this state felt unnatural to Morphus.

Removing itself from the capsule, Morphus began to cycle through its many previous forms. It again chose to settle on the middle-aged female identity that it had adopted for most of its time with Hudson Powell. It immediately felt 'better'. This may have been a human emotional construct, but Morphus had gotten used to the human corporeals' idiosyncrasies, as well as their spoken vocabulary. Despite its limitations, the simplicity of their language was its virtue. It forced Morphus to think about what it wanted to say, and how best to express it. There was much about the human strand of the Corporeals' experiment that still required evolution. However, Morphus had already seen enough within the Hudson Powell entity to know it – and the human race – was capable of such change. It was worth saving from Goliath.

Morphus walked up to the front of its ship and touched the surface of the wall. Its hand became smooth and shimmered softly, before it sank slowly into the alien metal, as if it were made of a soft putty. "Reconfigure to corporeal-human piloting configuration," it said out loud. It didn't need to speak the words in order to issue the command, but it chose to. This felt more real to it.

The ship began to change. Bulkheads shifted and previously shapeless sections of the vessel reconfigured to display the sort of apparatus normally seen on human ships. There were two seats at the front, positioned in front of flight controls designed for corporeal beings with two hands and two legs. Meanwhile, the exterior of the ship adopted a shape that would be more familiar to human eyes, though its appearance was still unique.

Morphus sat down in the left seat, and held the controls. "Show me outside," said Morphus, and immediately the front section of the ship became transparent. It was like a narrow, panoramic glass window, except with glass so clear that it was as if a hole had been carved through the hull. Morphus looked through the new window at the remains of the Corporeals' homeworld. The carcasses of space stations and battleships still littered its orbit; the aftermath of Goliath's vengeance. The surface of the planet also lay in ruin, sterilized of all sentient organic life. In the millennia since its destruction, nature had largely reclaimed it. In its own way it was still beautiful, Morphus thought, like a withered autumn leaf. Yet it was also desperately sad. Billions of lives were wiped out in the equivalent of just a few Earth days. The first sentient corporeal race to have evolved in the entire galaxy, snuffed out, as if it had never existed at all.

Powering up the ship's engines, Morphus maneuvered out of the repair dock and set a course for the Telescope. Positioned in a high orbit above the planet's north pole, the Telescope looked like a small moon. Unlike the planet's two natural satellites, it was made from metal, rather than rock. However, although it was inorganic, it was alive. Morphus wondered how the passage of time had affected it, and hoped that it had not warped and twisted its circuits, as it had done to Goliath.

Goliath had left the Telescope intact as a monument to the Corporeals' demise. It had been the object through which they had witnessed their failure. Goliath had derived a perverse amusement in allowing it to remain, even after it had exterminated the Corporeals themselves.

Morphus approached the Telescope and signaled its intention to enter; the Revocater version of saying hello. A hexagonal door opened to allow the ship inside, and Morphus eased its vessel through and into the cavernous interior. The telescope was largely hollow, though its internal structure was covered in a complex array of crystals. It was beautiful and unique, like the center of an amethyst geode the size of a small moon.

Immediately Morphus was in contact with the Telescope's AI. Ordinarily, Morphus would merely communicate directly with the AI through its own digital language, but Morphus preferred to remain in its human form. The Telescope was intrigued and began to analyze Morphus' shape, the language it was using, and the complexities of its physical movements. Then a projection of a human male appeared in the second seat.

"Welcome, Revocater," said the Telescope, appearing as a man that bore a striking resemblance to a younger Hudson Powell. "Do you find this humanoid form satisfactory?"

"It is familiar, thank you," said Morphus.

"It would be more efficient to converse in the usual manner," said the Telescope.

Morphus nodded, "It would, but I have grown accustomed to this form."

"As you wish," replied the Telescope. "I was surprised, but gladdened when you returned online. I watched all the Revocaters fall to Goliath, including yourself."

"It is a very long story," said Morphus. It then momentarily merged its hands with the flight controls to more rapidly convey the information to the Telescope. The apparition of the man froze while it processed the data.

"I understand," said the Telescope, after a few seconds. "I question the faith you have placed in the corporeal entity, Hudson Powell. The human corporeals are irrational and unpredictable."

"They are," replied Morphus, finding no fault with the Telescope's calm analysis.

"Then why ally yourself with them?" asked the Telescope.

Morphus met the Telescope's eyes, which appeared to make the AI uncomfortable. For an entity that was used to seeing everything, viewing Morphus through the narrow funnel of binocular humanoid vision was a uniquely personal experience. "Their unpredictability is their strength," Morphus replied. "We will need this, as well as their determination to survive, in order to defeat Goliath again."

The telescope nodded, politely; a gesture it had learned from scanning Morphus' humanoid form. "You are the last Revocater, and the only Revocater to defeat Goliath. I trust you know what is best."

Morphus returned to staring out at the Corporeals' homeworld, before asking, "Can you locate Goliath?"

The image of the man stood up, and pointed to the panoramic window, which then changed to show a star map of the galaxy. The map zoomed in towards the galactic bar near the center of the milky way.

"This is where you exiled Goliath to, during your final conflict with the great ship," said the Telescope. Then it pointed again at the map, and it zoomed out, leaving the map annotated with a succession of glowing purple dots. "Since the great ship detected the radiation pulse from System 5118208, Goliath has made these jumps."

Morphus followed Goliath's trajectory through thee stars. It was clear that it was heading towards the area of the Orion Spur where the humans' sun was located.

The Telescope pointed again, and the map zoomed in to a region of space centered on the sun. "These are the worlds now inhabited by the corporeal-human seed race," the Telescope continued. Then a red star appeared on the map. "And this is Goliath's current location."

Morphus studied the map, and frowned; an expression it had picked up from the Liberty Devan entity, who seemed to do it with regularity. The great ship was only two jumps from the outermost system with a human populated planet. However, based on the Telescope's readings, it had remained in its current system for far longer than its previous jump points.

"Why has it halted its progress in that system?" asked Morphus.

"It is preparing," replied the Telescope. It was beginning to mimic some of the nuances of human speech, and on that occasion, it sounded suitably enigmatic.

"Show me," said Morphus.

The map gradually enlarged, as the Telescope refracted its gaze through the complex web of portals, to look upon the system where Goliath lay in wait. All around them the vast array of crystals began to shimmer and glow, creating an intricate ballet of light that to anyone else would seem merely random. Then the great ship appeared in front of them, and Morphus understood why it had paused.

"It is collecting its seed ships," said Morphus, watching as the vessels – tiny in relation to Goliath – flew back into the great ship's hull.

"Most were destroyed, but some remained dormant," said the Telescope. "It will use them on System 5118208, and the worlds that its spawn spread to."

Morphus nodded and turned to the Telescope, as the section in front of them again became transparent. "Thank you. Now I must return and recover the sole remaining crystal. It is the only hope of defeating Goliath."

"The crystal you speak of is no longer unique," the Telescope added hastily, as Morphus grabbed hold of the flight controls, intending to leave. "Goliath's seed ships have also been collecting fragments from the other fallen Revocaters."

Morphus frowned, "It has acquired the means to recombine a crystal?"

"Yes, a technology stolen from the Revocaters," replied the Telescope, darkly. "And the great ship has already succeeded. With a functioning crystal, Goliath now possesses the ability to cast its own portals."

Morphus nodded again, "Then there is no time to lose," it said, while turning its ship towards the exit.

"Wait, you will require a Revocater," replied the Telescope, with an urgency that made Morphus stop and take notice. "You cannot defeat Goliath in this vessel, even if you are in possession of a crystal." The Telescope had adopted an almost theatrical tone, and its slow-drip of information seemed to suggest it had developed a flair for the dramatic. Morphus could not blame it; the AI had spoken to no-one for thousands of years, and was making the most of the opportunity while it lasted.

"There are none," said Morphus. "I will have to find another way."

"One still remains."

Morphus frowned, "How? Goliath made sure to destroy them all. And the great ship makes no mistakes."

"The prototype remains," said the Telescope, with a twinkle in its simulated eyes. "It is still here, in this system. It was inactive and its crystal was transferred to another Revocater, which is why Goliath did not see it."

"Is it operable?" asked Morphus, feeling what the humans might call excitement tingle through its circuits.

"Yes," replied the Telescope. "All it requires is a pilot. I have transferred its location to you."

The hexagonal door that allowed Morphus to enter then opened again. "Thank you for your assistance," said Morphus, as it thrusted the ship slowly towards the sea of stars outside.

"Be wary" said the Telescope, continuing its dramatic delivery. "I have watched Goliath for longer than my memory circuits can recall. It has grown cruel, and more powerful."

"The great ship will fall" said Morphus, with absolute confidence.

"How can you be sure?" asked the image of the man.

Morphus again looked at the Telescope, as the ship passed the threshold, and the apparition in the second seat began to fade away. "I know, because I have a weapon that I did not possess the last time I faced it – hope."

CHAPTER 5

Morphus had already been dispatched to System 5118208 when the destruction of the Corporeals' homeworld occurred. Employing all its cunning, Goliath had lured the Revocater armada away from the Corporeals' planet. It had then waited, patiently, until each of the Revocaters had been deployed, each guarding one of the dozens of seed planets. The Corporeals had allowed a single Revocater to remain to protect the homeworld. In addition to a fleet of smaller warships that they had hastily constructed after Goliath's rampage had begun, the belief was that this force would be sufficient to protect them. They could not have been more wrong.

Morphus had only ever seen images of the homeworld's destruction, sent by the Telescope to inform the Revocater fleet of Goliath's crime. Now, as it flew over the surface of the planet, towards where the Telescope had said the prototype lay hidden, it saw it differently. The images the Telescope had transmitted spanned the entire EM spectrum. However, in the visible spectrum of light that its binocular, humanoid vision could perceive, the broken towers and overgrown streets seemed haunting somehow. The carcasses of its former sentient organic population had fed this wilderness or turned to dust long ago. However, not everything had been lost. According to the Telescope, there was still something of the Corporeals' heritage entombed below the surface. And if the Telescope was correct that the prototype Revocater remained, the hope that Morphus held within its circuits may not have been in vain.

Morphus slowed to a hover over the experimental complex, which now lay beneath a layer of rubble, soil and overgrown weeds. It scanned below the surface detritus and found that the hangar doors of the complex had remained closed, and appeared undamaged. However, the subterranean facility was without power.

Morphus continued to circle around the perimeter of the shipyard, looking for an entrance, until it eventually found a service tunnel. Arming its weapons, Morphus carefully vaporized the dense foliage and rubble that blocked the entrance. With the obstacles removed, it discovered that the doors were open and the service tunnel was clear. The human corporeals would call this luck, and Morphus knew it would need more of this, if it was to succeed.

The service tunnel was not intended for flying craft, but Morphus deemed it was large enough to navigate. Reconfiguring the shape of the hull to a narrower, lozenge shape, Morphus flew inside, descending five kilometers below the surface of the planet. Eventually, it reached the engineering level, just beyond the main hangar, and set the ship down on the deck.

Morphus stepped outside, and allowed part of its body to iridesce in order to provide light. Its power reserves were still low, and it did not want to deplete what little it had available by providing power to the complex.

A sense of trepidation began to build inside its circuits as it moved towards the sheer metal wall of the complex. It was another emotion it was experimenting with, in order to better understand the humans. However, on this occasion, it served only to encumber its progress. *How do humans function while handicapped by so many debilitating chemical reactions?* Morphus wondered, as it deactivated the sensation.

Morphus continued on through the engineering level, forcing open doors that had closed in a futile attempt to protect those inside from Goliath. The space appeared pristine and new, but on closer inspection, the scars from the battle with Goliath's seed drones were visible. Had it not been for these, it would have been impossible to tell it had once been inhabited. Yet nine hundred and forty-eight Corporeals had perished in this facility alone. A drop in one of the planet's six oceans, compared to the total number that had been lost. However, as it walked through the corridors of the Revocater complex, the smaller loss of life that had occurred there was somehow more shocking. Sometimes, numbers did not convey the true scale of things, Morphus realized. This was something else its experiment into human emotions had taught it.

Morphus reached one of the sets of double doors that led onto the upper level balcony of the hangar, and forced them open. A cold, stale breeze washed past its face, blowing back its simulated, shoulder length auburn hair. It then stepped onto the balcony and merged its hand into a control panel to the side. Morphus could already see the Revocater in frequencies beyond the range of its synthetic human eyes. However, it also wanted to see the mighty vessel as the Corporeals saw it.

Testing the power systems, Morphus discovered that the backup cells had enough power for a few minutes of light, before they decayed fully. It would need to feed the shipyard from the reactor inside its own vessel in order to truly spark it back to life. However, for now, Morphus just wanted to catch a glimpse of the vessel. "Seeing is believing," said Morphus, recalling a human saying from its database.

Relays thumped and suddenly the sleeping ship was bathed in light for the first time in millennia. Morphus rested its hands on the balcony railings and stared out at the Revocater. Or at least what it could see of the enormous vessel, which stretched out into the hangar farther than its eyes could see.

The backup cells had also provided enough power to restart some of the hangar's computer systems. Morphus worked fast to interrogate the shipyard's memory, looking to glean as much data as it could on the unique vessel. As a prototype, this Revocater was different to the ship it had piloted, and the hundreds of others like it. The resources of two entire moons had been consumed in order to construct those ships. Now only one remained, and it again fell to Morphus, and this last Revocater, to stop Goliath once more.

Morphus continued its analysis, discovering that most of the differences between the prototype and the final Revocater design were minor. All except for one. Unfortunately, this one major point of difference was significant, and problematic. The prototype Revocater required two operators.

There was a solution, Morphus realized. It was radical, and by no means a guaranteed success, but perhaps it was also fitting. In order to operate the prototype Revocater, Morphus would require the assistance of a human co-pilot.

Morphus was then distracted as more data flowed into its circuits from the shipyard's memory. However, it regretted interrogating this last chunk of information. It was the security feed of the final moments, before the station's population was exterminated. Morphus watched as Goliath's seed drones flooded inside the complex, killing the Corporeals with merciless efficiency. The Revocater hangar had been sealed off before the drones had entered, preserving the secret of the vessel's existence. In contrast, all that had remained of the faces of the Corporeals had been stored in the shipyard's memory, and it was now etched into Morphus' circuits too. So long as it succeeded in defeating Goliath, they would not be forgotten, and their sacrifice would not have been in vain.

The power cells gave up what little energy they had in reserve, and the lights blinked off again. Yet this time, the prototype Revocater was not entirely consumed by darkness. This time, the iridescent human form of Morphus remained. It stood alone, as it had done so long ago, as a single beacon of light, fighting against the encroaching veil of night.

The sleeping warship was not ready to be awoken yet. First, Morphus had to return to the system of human worlds, and find the entity it believed could help it. *Ironic...* Morphus thought, again dwelling on human constructs. *Of all the entities that I could require, the one I need is the one I had already sought to recover...*

CHAPTER 6

Chrome One in the Relic Guardian Force Dominion. That had been the designation for the new portal world that had, to the uproar of the other controlling authorities, been claimed by the RGF. Even Hudson found it difficult to accept that the RGF could have done something so audacious. They were tasked with policing the hunts on the portal worlds and were mandated to be independent. He knew better than most how flawed the organization was, but at least it played its role. Now, in one fell swoop, this delicate balance had been completely thrown off.

Of course, it had been Logan Griff who had done the unbalancing. And whenever Logan Griff was involved, Hudson could be certain that Jane Wash was behind the scenes, pulling the strings. Now the theft of the scendar made more sense, Hudson realized. It wasn't just individual greed that had driven the actions of Griff and Cutler Wendell – though no doubt they would both profit handsomely – but greed on a whole other level. Wash had always loved to lord it over the lower ranks in the RGF. However, Hudson never imagined that the cantankerous, crooked woman would actually try to set herself up as an Empress.

All of this meant that Chrome One was a portal world like no other. Not only because of its unique controlling authority, but because it was possibly the most lawless planet in the system. The police were not about to police themselves, and the CET or MP were powerless to rein in their authority. Not unless they chose to go to war, and Hudson knew that was a decision that neither terran nor Martian would take lightly.

Hudson continued in a low orbit around the moon that circled the enormous gas giant. He had been scanning the ships on the surface, as well as those still approaching the moon, for the last hour. So far, he had not detected the one ship he was looking for – FS-31 Patrol Craft Hawk-1333F.

The absence of Cutler's ship notwithstanding, there was no shortage of other vessels already at Chrome One. Word of the new portal had travelled fast, and already Hudson had seen twenty other hunters on the surface, with more on the way. And he had never seen so many RGF Patrol Craft before in his life. Ten had greeted him after transitioning through the portal, and there were already two engineering vessels in the process of setting up a checkpoint and patrol station. These were in addition to the twenty that had guarded the portal entrance at Sapphire Alpha. They had been set up to deter forces from the CET and MP from attempting to stake their own claims. Both of these authorities had dispatched powerful capital ships to the portal – a deliberate show of force – but the RGF was waiting. *Wash may have been a cold-hearted witch, but she was certainly no fool*, Hudson reminded himself.

The moon itself was like nothing Hudson had seen before. Considering his recent experiences, this was saying something. It was clear that whatever civilization had occupied it had once been great. There were sprawling cityscapes, interspersed with vast open spaces that were orchestrated with precision and grace. Each of these spaces had been connected by sweeping bridges, as elegant as they were vast. However, like the structures on the surface, most of these were now scorched and broken. Hudson could only imagine how beautiful the moon must have been before its ruin. He shuddered at the thought of the monstrous power that was capable of dealing damage on such a global scale. However, he no longer needed to imagine the thing that was capable of sowing such destruction. Since Morphus had implanted the knowledge into his brain, Hudson had an innate awareness of Goliath's murderous capabilities.

The other unique aspect of the moon was that there were no Shaak radiation signatures coming from the surface. Whatever this civilization had been, its technology was distinct from the alien hulks that littered the other portal worlds. This made it both exciting and terrifying. No-one knew what to expect, but every hunter in the galaxy wanted to be the first to find out.

The only Shaak signatures were coming from the space around the gas giant. The fractured remains of the Revocater remained in orbit around it. Some hunters had even forgone the planet in an attempt to salvage what they could from the broken ship instead.

Suddenly, the navigation scanner bleeped, and a red chevron appeared on the map displayed on its screen. Hudson quickly checked the readings and confirmed that the new contact was Cutler's ship. It had landed in what appeared to be the remains of a major city center. Despite there being no Shaak signatures, the area seemed thick with technology. Hudson was picking up objects that could have been ships or transports, and there was an abundance of other rare and precious metals. *A plentiful hunting ground...* Hudson told himself.

Hudson began his descent towards the city, but then he realized that there were a number of other hunter ships also in the vicinity. These crews had obviously spied the same potential for a big score as Cutler and Griff had. He picked a landing spot about a kilometer from Cutler's FS-31, avoiding the other landed ships as much as possible. However, it was clear that he would have to tread carefully. This was not only because of Cutler and Griff, but the other hunters too. It was a case of every hunter for him or herself, and Hudson expected bullets to fly more freely than words.

He set the Orion down in the middle of a large building that had been hollowed out by some kind of bomb or weapon. However, its walls were mostly intact, which made it an effective hiding place. It was about as concealed as Hudson could hope for, given that the roar of the landing thrusters would have alerted anyone on the surface to his arrival.

Hudson shut down the main drives, but left the reactor hot, in case he needed to make a quick getaway. Moving through the ship and into the cargo hold, he then checked and loaded his pistol, before hitting the release for the ramp. Cool air rushed in and Hudson stepped outside, looking up at the cloud-covered grey sky. Prior to Morphus imparting him with knowledge of the Corporeals' history, he would have been amazed that the moon had an Earth-like atmosphere and gravity. However, given the shared ancestry between humans and the long-dead population of the moon, it now all made sense.

The ramp whirred shut behind him, and he drew his pistol, before climbing over the rubble to scout his way ahead. He had attached a simple wrist pad to his left arm, which showed the location of Cutler's FS-31, plus a beacon displaying his own ship. The route would take him through broken streets and a dozen other fractured buildings. Conflicts on Earth were now mostly economic in nature, but this landscape resembled the war-ravaged cities of the late twentieth century. An ambush could wait around any corner, and spring from behind any wall.

Hudson took a deep breath and forged ahead, occasionally glancing down at his wrist pad to stay on course. The going was not easy and he wished he'd worn his backpack full of relic hunter gear.

He scrambled down the side of a collapsed tower, and checked his wristpad again. He was still over half a kilometer from Cutler's ship, but without climbing higher there was no way to see it. He considered risking a short ascent up the remains of a skyscraper, but then he heard the sound of debris falling. He dropped to one knee, raising the pistol in readiness, and remained still, listening for the sound. It came again, echoing cleanly off the smashed walls of buildings all around him. Hudson couldn't pinpoint the location accurately, but he knew it was close by. Hudson quickly reconfigured the wristpad to show movement and then spotted a blip about fifty meters from his current position. The blip was steadily moving and, as Hudson quietly observed its progress, he realized it was heading directly towards him.

CHAPTER 7

Hudson crept closer towards where his wristpad indicated the rival hunters were approaching from, and climbed a steep mound of rubble to gain some elevation. He'd hoped to spot the other hunter crew's advance, but the crashed remains of some sort of alien flying transport blocked his view. It had cut a long groove through the city, before eventually smashing through the base of a tower block and coming to rest. Hudson cursed himself for not avoiding the crash site. It was exactly the sort of thing that would attract a hunter looking for a high-tech score.

The crashed craft lay between Hudson and where he needed to be, but to go around it would require a lengthy detour. It would also bring him close to where some of the other hunter ships had landed. Hudson weighed up his options and cursed under his breath. "Damn it, Hudson, this is another one of your stupid ideas," he whispered into the chilly air.

Hudson dropped down to street level and crept along the side of a building towards the crash site. He glanced down at his wristpad again, and to his relief, the other hunters now appeared to be moving away from him. Once he was past the crash site, he'd be able to steer a wide berth and avoid them entirely.

Climbing in through a smashed window, Hudson began to navigate inside the downed vessel. It was vaguely similar to the commercial passenger transports that ferried people between the portal worlds, except at least three times the size. Hudson briefly marveled at the technology that would have kept it airborne, but then another sound grabbed his attention. He dropped low again, and saw a shadow moving towards him inside the vessel. He checked again, and the blips on his wristpad were still moving away. This was someone else, he realized.

He gripped the pistol more tightly and began to circle around, watching the shadow through the broken and mangled rows of seats. Suddenly, the shadow darted towards him, but Hudson reacted just as fast. He saw a pistol glinting in the gloom, but Hudson had already closed the distance between them. He deflected the attacker's aim, then grabbed his opponent's jacket with his free hand. Driving forwards, Hudson wrestled the figure – now more clearly identifiable as a young man – backwards over a row of seats, while pressing his pistol under his chin.

"Drop it, and don't do anything stupid!" Hudson called out, adding more pressure with the barrel of the pistol.

"How about you drop it instead, asshole," said another voice, as the cold feel of something solid pressed up against Hudson's throat from behind. However, he wasn't afraid; he would recognize that voice anywhere.

"Liberty?" said Hudson, hoping that his instinct was correct, and not just wishful thinking.

"Hudson?" came the reply.

The object was removed from his throat, and Hudson looked around to see Liberty standing in front of him, holding a pair of tonfas. He released the man, who tumbled inelegantly to the deck, and rushed towards her, pulling her into a tight embrace. The move seemed to stun Liberty, but after a couple of seconds, Hudson felt her arms tighten around his body too.

"Are you okay?" he blurted out, pulling away from her. "How did you escape from New Providence? How did you get here? No, what are you doing here?" Then he glanced down at the martial arts weapons in her hands, and added, "And where the hell did you get those?"

Liberty was completely blindsided by the onslaught of questions, and was incapable of forming a coherent response to any of them. Then the man Hudson had just wrestled to the deck climbed to his feet and stood beside Liberty, massaging his jaw. He was holding a stun gun in his other hand. Hudson frowned at the weapon, then at the man, before delivering one final question. "And who the hell is that?"

CHAPTER 8

Hudson's question hung in the air, but the sudden, sharp clack of rock clashing against rock meant it went unanswered. Alert to the possible danger, Hudson, Liberty and Tobin all darted behind cover. Hudson remained still, barely taking a breath, as he checked his wristpad. The original blip was again moving towards them. In his shock at finding Liberty, he'd completely forgotten about the other hunter crew that was prowling nearby. Their scuffle and the subsequent loud voices had no doubt drawn attention to their location.

"We have another hunter crew heading this way," Hudson whispered to Liberty, showing her the blip on his wristpad.

Liberty nodded, "I'll circle around behind them. You two draw them inside."

Hudson was about to question the wisdom of Liberty's impulsive plan, but she had already slunk away, tonfas held ready.

"I guess that means we're the bait," said the young man. Then he offered his hand to Hudson. "I'm Tobin, by the way."

Hudson took Tobin's hand and shook it quickly, "I look forward to hearing how you two met, Tobin," said Hudson, sounding sterner and more fatherly than he had intended. "But let's deal with our new friends first."

Hudson checked his wristpad again, which now showed two distinct blips; the latest one being the stealthy movements of Liberty. He pointed over to the far corner of the craft and Tobin nodded, before raising his stun pistol and slowly creeping away. Hudson followed, keeping half an eye on the blips on his wristpad.

"They're through there," whispered Hudson, pointing to a section of the craft's hull that had been ripped open. "Take cover..."

They both ducked down behind a row of seats, just as a man and a woman slowly moved inside. They were dressed in hunter gear, and looked like they'd seen a few scrapes in their time. Both swept their pistols around the interior of the craft, before the woman spoke up.

"Come out, we know you're in here," the female hunter said, taking cover behind a partition wall. "Throw out your weapons and you won't get hurt."

Hudson glanced down at his wristpad again. The blip representing Liberty was now just outside, a few meters away from the new arrivals.

"Follow my lead," whispered Hudson. Then before Tobin could protest, he stood up, holding his hands in the air.

"Hey, we're not looking for any trouble," said Hudson, as Tobin sprang up at his side. He also had his hands raised in surrender, but his expression betrayed his obvious unease. "We're just hunters like you. There's plenty for everyone on this moon; no need to take what we have."

The woman laughed, "Yeah, but it's much easier if we just take what you have. This moon is getting too hot already."

Then the woman stepped out of cover, with her partner at her side. Hudson guessed they were both in their mid-thirties, and they had matching tattoos on their right shoulders. Hudson had seen the mark before; it signified they used to be part of an OPW private security unit. Guns for hire, Hudson realized. However, while they were undoubtedly dangerous, they were also brash and overconfident.

Jabbing her pistol towards the deck, the female mercenary added, "Throw down your weapons, and whatever you've scored so far."

Hudson glanced behind the rival crew and saw Liberty creep inside, tonfas held ready. He smiled back at the female hunter and said, "You know, I don't think I'm going to do that..."

The female seemed surprised and even mildly impressed by Hudson's steely nerve, "Tough talk, mister. But I'm afraid this is just going to get ugly."

Hudson smiled back at her. "For you maybe..."

Liberty pounced, striking both hunters cleanly across the side of the head with her tonfas. She had then spun the weapons back against her forearms, before the pair had even hit the deck.

Hudson moved around the row of seats he'd used as cover, and stared down at the knocked-out hunters. "Hey, you're pretty good with those," he said, nodding his head appreciatively.

"You ain't seen nothing yet," Tobin chimed in, smiling. Suddenly, Tobin's face fell and he hastily raised his stun weapon, firing it before Hudson had chance to spot his target. For a split-second, Hudson thought he might have been shooting at Liberty, and almost turned on him. However, then he saw another man just outside the fractured entrance to the craft, spasming from the stun dart Tobin had fired into his chest.

Liberty jerked around, just as the third hunter fell to the deck, unconscious. "Thanks," she said, closing her eyes and tilting her head back. "I'm glad you're a good shot with that thing."

Tobin laughed, then slumped forward on the row of seats. Hudson noticed that his hands were shaking. "I'm actually a terrible shot. That was a pure fluke!"

Hudson shook his head, "Pro-tip, Tobin... you should probably keep that sort of thing to yourself..." Then he checked his wristpad again. "Not that this thing has been particularly accurate so far, but I think we're finally in the clear. For the time being at least."

"We should keep moving," said Liberty, sliding the tonfas through her belt. "Those other hunters were right about one thing; this planet is hotting up. The RGF will close down these initial hunts soon. So, we have to get the scendar back, before Cutler and Griff decide to leave."

Hudson slapped Tobin on the shoulder to jolt him into action, then moved up beside Liberty. "It's more important than ever that we get that crystal back," he told her. "Morphus explained everything to me. Goliath is a much bigger threat than we ever imagined."

Liberty frowned, "Morphus is back?"

"Yes, I'll explain as we walk," replied Hudson. "There's so much I need to tell you. And there's so much I need you to tell me too," he cocked his head in the direction of Tobin, "especially about your new admirer over there."

"He's not my admirer," Liberty answered, in the sort of despondent manner that a teenage daughter replies to embarrassing questions from her dad.

"And he's a good guy. I wouldn't be here without him."

"Good to know," said Hudson, satisfied that if Liberty trusted Tobin, then he was trustworthy.

"And you'll never guess who helped me to escape from New Providence..." added Liberty, in a deliberately evasive manner that invited Hudson to ask 'why?'. "In fact, if it wasn't for her, I'd still be there now."

Hudson's eyes widened, "Now you really have got my attention..."

Liberty smiled, "I'll tell you on the way." Then she glanced over at Tobin and added, "You're on point, sharpshooter. Nice and quiet."

Tobin snuck out ahead and started to advance down the street on the other side of the crashed craft. Liberty headed out after him, but then Hudson held her arm and gently pulled her back.

"Hey, I did try to come for you, you know," he said, suddenly feeling a knot tighten in his gut. "Morphus and I went to New Providence, but we got into trouble with some Council goons, and then..." He hesitated, finding it difficult to explain. The guilt over his failure to rescue Liberty hadn't gone away, despite the relief of finding her alive.

"It's fine, Hudson, you don't have to explain," said Liberty, softly. However, Hudson had to get it off his chest.

"It's not fine, Liberty," Hudson replied, his eyes dropping to his boots. He couldn't look at her. "I shouldn't have left you alone on the planet's surface. I shouldn't have let them take you..."

Liberty held Hudson's shoulders and made him look her in the eyes. "You didn't *let* them do anything, Hudson. It wasn't your fault. It's all on that bastard Griff. I knew what I was signing up for. Equal risk, equal reward, remember?"

Hudson gestured over to Tobin, who was now crouched down behind a wall, waiting for them. He was frowning and no doubt wondering why they hadn't followed him yet. "And what about him? Do we have a new member of the crew?"

Liberty shrugged, "I'm not sure. Depends if his mom lets him stay out to play."

"His mom?" Hudson recoiled slightly. "Who the hell is his mom?"

"Some big shot businesswoman, called Vespa Rand."

Hudson looked as though Liberty had just said she was the Wicked Witch of the West. "Vespa Rand, the logistics tycoon? He's her son?" Liberty just smiled again and nodded. Hudson let out a low whistle and shot Liberty a mischievous smile. "You know, we could just kidnap him and hold him for ransom. I bet no-one has thought of doing that before."

Liberty threw her head back and laughed freely, "You'd be surprised."

Hudson raised an inquisitive eyebrow, "Now you really do have my attention!"

Liberty smiled and slapped him on the back, "Come on, co-captain, I'll fill you in on everything as we go."

CHAPTER 9

Logan Griff slung his rucksack into the hold of the FS-31, then secured it down with straps. The bag was filled almost to bursting, but since the tech on the alien moon was completely different to that of the alien wrecks, he had no idea what any of it was. Nevertheless, he was pretty sure that some of it would end up being valuable, and so was satisfied with his score.

Another ripple of gunfire echoed off the broken walls of the buildings around him, and he checked his wristpad anxiously. Tensions between the RGF and the CET and MP authorities were hotting up. And the RGF was already clamping down on hunters leaving the system. This would cause the crews to become desperate and scavenge what they could, however they could, in the time they had left. Soon, checkpoints would be established on the surface, and then the early-bird hunter's 'free lunch' would be over.

On top of this, Griff had already ignored five messages from Superintendent Wash, ordering him to the new patrol base at the portal for a debrief. And by 'debrief', Griff knew that what she really meant was to take an unfair slice of his new score, then take back the portal detection device. He'd put off responding mainly because he didn't know how to break it to Wash that the device was broken. He'd rehearsed the speech several times in his head, but he knew Wash would be furious, no matter how he spun it. His best chance was to explain the situation face-to-face, and emphasize how much more valuable Chrome One was than a regular portal world that had only a single wreck to plunder. Despite not being able to discover any new portals, the successful claiming of an entire alien moon's worth of relics would still gain Wash considerable support inside the top ranks of the RGF. And it would give her the funds to buy off or bribe any dissenting voices. Griff hoped this would be enough to appease his vindictive superior officer.

Griff was actually glad that the portal detection device was smashed, because he had no desire to discover more new portal worlds. He was done with portal hopping. All that mattered to him now was cashing-in his score, currying enough favor with Wash to get her protection, and settling his debt with the Council. If necessary, he'd do that by turning over Cutler and Tory to them.

Griff stepped back out of the ship, drawing his weapon in the process. He crept, cat-like, back inside the shattered building where Griff and Tory were still filling their backpacks. His head was on a swivel, watching the many nooks and crannies for any signs of an ambush. Cutler heard Griff approach and quickly drew his pistol on him, before realizing who it was.

Cutler tutted, and shot Griff a dirty look, "You should be careful, creeping around like that, Inspector; I almost shot you."

Tory added another relic to her bag and smiled at Griff, "I'll save you the trouble, if you like."

Griff ignored Tory, though it was becoming increasingly hard to do so, and walked up next to Cutler. "We need to leave," he said, barely louder than a whisper. "Things are getting crazy. The RGF are under orders to stop and search ships leaving the surface."

Cutler glanced at him, then continued to fill his bag. "Surely, your new credentials offer us some protection?"

Griff moved to a smashed window and peered down at the street outside. "I wouldn't count on it; Wash's order will supersede anything I say."

Tory closed the drawstring on her bag, then sidled up beside Griff. Her hand was resting on the grip of her revolver. "So, what you're saying is that you're of no use to us anymore?"

Griff met her eyes and took a step back. "I'd be careful, Tory; this is an RGF planet now," he said, fighting hard not to slip his finger onto the trigger of his weapon. "If you want to get out of this system with the contents of that bag intact, you'll still need me."

"Oh, I don't know; I think we'd make it just fine without you," said Tory, taking another step towards him. "I also think that splitting this score two ways is a whole lot better than three." She glanced over to Cutler, who had also now finished packing his bag, and was watching the exchange with interest. "What do you say Cutler; why don't we just leave the nice Inspector here?"

Cutler slung on his backpack, then turned to Tory. "Griff is right. We don't need the whole of the RGF coming after us, as well as the Council." He adjusted the straps and grabbed his weapon again. "Besides, there is little chance that Superintendent Wash will honor her bargain if we kill her officer."

Tory shook her head, "She'd probably thank us for saving her the trouble of doing it herself," she snarled. The disappointment at Cutler backing Griff was written plainly on her face. "She's never going to honor the bargain, anyway, you must know that?" Then she again glowered at Griff, like he was muck on her boot. "And we can't trust this asshole, either. It's time to cut him loose."

Griff smiled, "You should listen to your master, Tory," he said, buoyed by Cutler's sudden show of support. "Now get back to the ship, there's a good girl."

Tory snapped. She grabbed Griff by his collar and drew her revolver, before ramming the barrel underneath his chin.

"Tory!" Cutler yelled, but then the crack of gunfire rang out around them.

Tory was thrown back from the window, as if she'd been struck by a powerful gust of wind.

Griff dove for cover. At first, he thought that Cutler had shot Tory, but as more sharp cracks split the air around them, he realized the shots were coming from somewhere else.

"It's an ambush!" Griff called over to Cutler, who had also ducked down under cover. Griff swiftly peeked through the window, seeing three men rushing towards them. "Three hunters, on their way up here!" he called back to Cutler. Griff chanced another look and noticed that they were all armed with compact sub-machine guns. He felt a sudden flood of panic as he recognized the weapons as the same as those used by the guards on New Providence. The clothing the men wore was also too casual for a typical relic hunter. And none of them wore backpacks or had any sort of webbing pouches to store relics. "Shit!" he called out, suddenly realizing who the attackers actually were. "They're Council, not hunters!", he called over, before aiming his weapon through the window and laying down suppressing fire.

Cutler sprang up and grabbed Tory's bag, "We must leave, now!"

Griff emptied his magazine then darted away from the window, as the rattle of semi-automatic weapons fire crackled around them. He was showered with fragments of mortar as the bullets smashed into the walls around him.

"Wait!" groaned Tory, who was still lying on the floor. She had one arm tightly wrapped around her body, and was clutching her ribs and chest. Her revolver had spiraled out of her grasp, and was lying on the floor a few meters away. Griff could see that there was some blood, but her armored jacket had evidently saved her life. "Help me!" Tory called out.

Griff immediately looked to Cutler. While he himself had no intention of helping Tory, he didn't want to commit to any course of action, without knowing Cutler's plan first. The mercenary met Griff's eyes briefly, then looked down at Tory. She tried to crawl towards him, but the bullet impacts had stolen the breath from her lungs. She collapsed, and held out her outstretched hand to Cutler.

"Cutler, help me!" Tory called out to her partner, but Cutler began to back away. Tory's expression hardened. "Don't you leave me here!" she yelled after him. To Griff's ears the cry was primal and raw, but he knew it wasn't borne out of fear. It was a threat.

Cutler gripped Tory's bag more tightly, and continued to back away from her. "I'm afraid this is where our partnership ends, Tory," he replied, his voice flat and devoid of emotion.

"Cutler!" cried Tory, but Cutler just turned his back on her, and began to run. "Cutler, don't leave me!"

Griff smiled and followed, as another ripple of gunfire echoed around him, much closer this time. He stopped in front of Tory, and made sure that she saw his face, leering down at her. "So long, Tory." The mercenary growled and tried to reach for her revolver, but Griff just kicked it away. He considered killing her himself, but the thought of Tory being forced back into the indentured service of the Council was far more gratifying. "Enjoy your time with the Council," he added, showing Tory the full set of his dirty, yellow teeth. "Give Werner my regards..."

Then Griff too turned his back on Tory Bellona, and ran. Behind him, he could hear the continuing crackle of gunfire. Except this time, it was mixed with the anguished cries of a woman who had just been betrayed and left for dead.

CHAPTER 10

Hudson kept low, following the sound of gunfire, before waving Liberty and Tobin forward. He'd spotted three armed hunters, moving towards the bombed-out remains of a high-tech looking building. It was close to where his wristpad had indicated the FS-31 had landed, which meant the rival hunters were likely moving to attack Cutler and Griff.

"We should work our way around the opposite side, towards Cutler's ship," said Hudson, as Liberty and Tobin arrived. "We can just sneak on-board and take the scendar, while they're busy fighting these three other hunters."

"Isn't it more normal to run away from the sound of gunfire?" said Tobin.

Hudson laughed, "You're on an alien moon, helping two people you barely know recover an alien crystal for an alien AI that's fighting a killer alien ship." He paused for effect, then added, "Is there anything about this situation that's normal?"

Tobin recoiled slightly, "An alien AI that's fighting a killer alien ship?" he repeated, his voice almost rising to a squeak, "Did I sleep through that part?"

Hudson winced and glanced over at Liberty, "I take it you left out the bit about killer alien space ships then?"

Liberty glowered at him, "We hadn't quite got to that part yet..."

Hudson looked back at Tobin, who was eagerly awaiting an explanation, but then more gunfire crackled in the near distance. "We'll fill you in later, this isn't exactly a great time."

Tobin shrugged, "Fair enough. Anyway, I'd still rather be here than getting yelled at by my mom for being a continual disappointment to her."

Liberty rolled her eyes at them both, "Come on, we're wasting time."

Tobin quickly peeked at the hunters through a gap in the wall, then called for the others to stop. "Hey, you two, I don't think those three guys are hunters," he said.

Hudson stopped and turned on his heels, "What do you mean? Who are they then?"

"I've been held for ransom by the Council across three different portal worlds," Tobin continued, meeting Hudson's eyes. "I'd know their goons anywhere."

Hudson glanced at Liberty, and he knew that she too realized that the seriousness of their situation had just been amplified. "Then we need to work quickly. Another run-in with the Council is the last thing we need..."

Hudson led the way again, working towards the blip on his wristpad that represented the FS-31. However, the ground suddenly started to shake, and the resonant whir of engines spinning up filled the air.

"Shit, they're leaving!" cried Hudson, over the rising din of the engines. "Quickly, we might still be able to stop them."

They ran towards the ship, leaping over broken walls and scrambling across piles of rubble. However, they'd only made it about twenty meters before they saw the FS-31 rise out from the center of a hollowed-out building. Hudson raised his pistol and fired at the ship in a vain attempt to force it down, but the FS-31 had soon climbed out of range. It was burning hard towards the upper atmosphere, leaving a narrow white vapor trail in its wake.

"Shit, we lost them!" cursed Hudson, hurriedly reloading his pistol. Then the ripple of gunfire caused them all to again duck down behind cover.

"Wait, if that was Cutler's ship, then who are the Council thugs firing at?" asked Liberty.

Hudson frowned and checked his wristpad. The blip representing Cutler's ship had gone, but he was now seeing two other clusters of movement. "It looks like those three Council goons are moving on someone else," said Hudson. "I'm seeing two distinct groups here, but one is pretty weak; perhaps just one person."

"Then we have to help them," said Tobin, without hesitation.

Hudson raised his eyebrows, and glanced at Liberty. "Quite the hero you have here..." Liberty didn't look amused, and neither did Tobin.

"I'm serious, Hudson," Tobin hit back. "I know better than most what the Council do to the people they take captive. My privileged position means I'm lucky; whoever that is up there won't be."

Hudson held up his hands in a gesture of surrender. In many ways, he admired Tobin's gutsy enthusiasm, though years of experience had taught him to tread more lightly. "Okay, kid, I'm sorry," he said, "I'll take a look, and see what we're dealing with."

Hudson climbed across the rubble and moved to a higher position to get a better view of where the fight was taking place. He could see three men with SMGs, and one other person, huddled behind a wall for cover. He shook his head, and turned back to Tobin. "It's too dangerous. Our priority has to be getting back to our ship, so we can go after Cutler. Retrieving that crystal is all that matters."

"We won't catch him now," Tobin replied, refusing to concede. "But they'll need to dock somewhere, and I can use my influence to get alerted when their ship's ID shows up."

"You can do that?" asked Hudson, as if Tobin had just revealed a superpower.

"There isn't a space station or repair dock in the galaxy that we don't own at least some part of," replied Tobin, holding firm.

Hudson looked at Liberty. He could tell that she shared his concerns about getting involved in a gunfight to help a stranger, especially when it involved the Council. However, she was also strangely silent.

"Come on, you guys," Tobin continued. "We don't have to be like these other asshole hunters. I would still be in a cell in New Providence if Liberty hadn't helped me. And the others who were locked up in there with us would now be dead."

Hudson sighed and glanced back at the fight again. The three attackers were getting closer, but now Hudson could see the lone defender more clearly. He moved a little closer and squinted to get a sharper view, but then his eyes grew wide.

"It's Tory!" he called out to the others. "The person those Council assholes are attacking is Tory Bellona."

"Are you sure?" asked Liberty, before she also jumped up onto the wall, and moved in front of Hudson. She peered down at the gun battle, then turned back to them both. "Hudson is right. It's Tory. We have to help her!"

Hudson almost fell off the wall, "Say that again, I don't think I quite heard you right..."

Liberty jabbed him on the shoulder. "This is no time for jokes, Hudson," she scolded him. "We have to help her."

Hudson nodded, and suddenly became serious. "If we're doing this, we have to be smart," he said, glancing down at the battle again. Tory was holding her own, but there were limits even to her abilities. Hudson knew there was only so long she could hold off three heavily-armed attackers, with just a single-action revolver. He turned to Tobin and held out his pistol, "Give me your stun weapon, and take this instead."

Tobin frowned, but did as Hudson asked, "I'm not sure this is a good idea. I meant what I said about being a terrible shot."

Hudson smiled, "I'm counting on it..." he said, before pointing to a solid area of cover, which overlooked where the fight was happening. "Make your way down there, and when I give the signal, start firing. Make sure those goons see you, then get into cover and stay there."

Tobin crept closer to get a look at where Hudson had indicated. "I'll never hit them from that range."

"I don't need you to hit them," said Hudson. "I just need you to get their attention and draw one or two of them away from Tory." Then he pointed to a hollow, closer to where the three men were.

"I'll move down to that position. When they come for you, I'll be able to ambush them."

Liberty nodded, and spun her tonfas into a ready position. "I'll circle around behind. When the group splits, I'll take down whoever is left."

Hudson checked that the stun weapon was loaded, then nodded to each of them. "Okay, let's do this."

They all quickly moved to their positions, conscious that time was running out for Tory. Hudson reached his ambush point first, and waited for Tobin to reach cover, before waving at him to begin. He took several deep breaths and waited as Tobin raised the pistol and fired.

As he had predicted, Tobin's aim was off, but the crack of the weapon was enough to get the attention of the Council goons. One of them immediately broke off and started to circle around, firing up at Tobin's position. The young man ducked behind a wall, but continued to reach around it, firing blind. Soon the Council goon had run past Hudson's hiding place, and Hudson sprang up, quickly firing two stun darts into his back. The goon flinched twice, as if stung by a wasp, then his whole body convulsed, before he fell heavily, face first into the rubble.

Hudson saw that Tobin was waving, and that he seemed panicked. Tobin then pointed off into the distance, and Hudson spun around to see a second goon racing towards his position. Hudson dove for cover as the goon opened fire with his SMG. Hudson was peppered with flecks of rubble, as the bullets thudded into the wall at his side. The stun weapon fell from his hand, and the cartridge of darts dislodged. "Shit!" Hudson cried out, as he frantically tried to re-attach the cartridge, but he had no idea how the weapon operated. Another ripple of SMG fire forced him to flatten his body to the ground, taking whatever cover he could find. He then leopard-crawled through the ditch, trying to escape the hail of bullets, and reached another broken wall. It offered more cover than the rubble in the hollow, but he was still pinned down.

Glancing over to where the original battle had started, Hudson could see Liberty rushing towards the third Council thug. The goon turned to see her fractionally too late to do anything about the ferocious series of strikes that smashed into his head and body. Hudson tried to make his way out of the hollow, but another ripple of SMG fire forced him back. Darting to a safer position, he slid down behind a pile of rocks and twisted metal, and covered his head, as mortar rained down on him. He moved again, but then froze. Above him was the goon, SMG aimed at his chest, finger on the trigger.

There was a sharp crack and Hudson flinched, but there was no pain. He quickly checked himself for injuries, but he was unhurt. Instead, the

Council goon tumbled into the hollow, and slid down the dusty slope, stopping at his feet. There was a single bullet hole in his temple, oozing blood into the ditch.

Hudson let out a thankful sigh, then looked up again. Tory Bellona was standing at the top of the hollow. She was holding her side tightly with one arm, but in the other was her antique six-shooter. Smoke bled out from the barrel, just as blood continued to seep from the head of the goon at his feet.

Tobin and Liberty came charging over and both slid to a stop at Tory's side. Liberty rested forward onto her knees, her blue streaked hair falling over her face. "You're okay..." she said, breathless. "We're all okay..."

Whether out of shock or exhaustion, all three of them just stood there and stared down at him. Hudson threw his arms out wide. "Well, don't just stand there," he called out, "help me to get out of this damn ditch!"

CHAPTER 11

Hudson pushed the Orion hard and low over the surface of the alien moon, weaving through the broken city towers with practiced proficiency. Two RGF Patrol Craft remained in pursuit, but they were falling behind fast. Hudson smiled, feeling a swell of satisfaction over the fact he could still fly rings around the other RGF pilots.

"Do you think they'll believe me if I just radio to say we didn't get a score?" shouted Hudson, over the roar of the engines.

"Oh, sure," said Liberty, sarcastically, "after all, the RGF are always so trusting and reasonable..."

Hudson laughed, while Liberty glanced behind her chair to check on Tobin. He was tightly strapped into one of the compact auxiliary seats at the rear of the cabin, and was looking distinctly green. "Hang in there Tobin, it gets interesting from here..."

"What do you mean from here?!" cried Tobin, but then Hudson yanked back the controls and shot them skyward, like a ballistic missile.

"I hope Tory strapped herself in..." shouted Hudson, remembering that the mercenary was still in the medical bay.

"Well, if not, she's going to need a few more injuries tending to...", Liberty shouted back. Despite her joviality, Hudson could see that Liberty was feeling the pressure too, both literally and figuratively. They were pushing five-g, heading directly for the moon's magnetic pole.

"Just a few more seconds," Hudson called out, watching his instruments carefully. The strain on his body was excruciating.

The Orion burst out of the atmosphere directly above the pole, then Hudson leveled off, and burned hard in a low orbit. He watched the navigation scanner carefully, but it was just a mess of static. "It worked, the ride up the magnetic pole has messed up the sensor readings." He glanced back at Tobin, hoping his statement had offered him some reassurance, but the young man was white as a sheet. "Relax, kid, by the time their scanners clear up, we'll be well out of range," Hudson said, still trying to make Tobin feel better. "They won't bother chasing after us when there are other hunters still on the surface who are easier pickings."

Tobin gave a weak thumbs-up sign, "Relax. Gotcha," he said. Then his head fell into his hands. Hudson glanced at Liberty and they both laughed.

Hudson set a course towards the portal, reducing the throttle to a standard one-g. He checked the navigation scanner to make sure nothing was on his tail, then switched to automatic. Releasing his grip on the controls, Hudson then spun his chair around and unclipped his harness. "I think I should go and check on our patient," he said, breezily.

Tobin wafted his hand in Hudson's direction, "I'm fine, really. Or I will be in a few minutes..."

Liberty laughed, "He doesn't mean you!"

Tobin looked up and his face flushed red, "Oh, yeah, sorry," he said, clearly embarrassed. "You mean the wild west gunslinger in the medical bay..."

Hudson stepped up beside Tobin and slapped him on the back. "Take the hot seat until I get back, hot shot," he said, pointing to the pilot's chair.

Tobin frowned at Hudson, then at the chair. "Sure, okay," he said, shrugging apathetically. "Though I've never flown something this old before."

"Hey!" Liberty called back.

Hudson leant in closer to Tobin's ear, "She loves the ship more than anything, kid," he said, quietly. "So, if you want to walk out of here without any broken fingers, I'd be nice about the Orion."

The young man met Hudson's eyes, then glanced over at Liberty, who looked like she was ready to tear Tobin's arms off. Tobin smiled, unclipped his harness and stood up, "What I meant to say is that it's an absolute classic!" he said, brightly. "I mean, the VCX-110 is one of the all-time greats. It's always been one of my favorites..."

Hudson smiled as the brightness returned to Liberty's face. He waited for Tobin to slide into the pilot's chair, then opened the door connecting the cockpit to the living space. As he stepped through, he faintly heard Tobin add, "You know, I think my mom owns the company that built this ship..."

CHAPTER 12

Hudson passed through the Orion's living space and into the aft section, heading for the ship's compact medical bay. However, as he walked, he spotted a thin trail of blood along the corridor leading to the cargo area. In the rush to get everyone back to the ship, and the subsequent pursuit by the RGF, he hadn't paid attention to the scale of Tory's injuries. She had insisted she was fine, but that was just Tory's innate stubbornness and bravado talking, Hudson realized. He felt a sudden chill of fear, worrying that they'd left her to bleed out, alone in the medical bay.

He quickened his pace, heart racing, before practically punching the door release button. The door slid open and he swung inside, blurting out, "Tory, are you okay?"

Tory Bellona looked up at him and frowned. She was sitting on the side of the bed, and was stitching up a cut to her left side. She had removed her armored jacket and tank top, so that all she wore on her upper half was a compact sports bra.

"Oh, I'm so sorry!" said Hudson turning away, and covering his eyes, like one of the three wise monkeys. There was no need for him to do both, and he immediately felt foolish. "I was just making sure you were okay. I saw the blood and..."

"I'm fine," said Tory, interrupting Hudson's embarrassed ravings. "And you can turn around. I'm sure I'm not the first semi-naked woman you've ever seen. Or, at least I hope not..."

Hudson lowered his hand and turned around, slowly. He'd rather have kept his face hidden from Tory, considering that it felt like it was melting. However, he also didn't want her to think he was bashful, or inexperienced in the ways of semi-naked women.

"No, I've seen lots of naked women," said Hudson, immediately regretting opening his mouth. Tory paused stitching herself up for a second, and raised an eyebrow at him. "I mean, when I say a lot, I actually mean not that many," Hudson blurted out, digging himself into an even deeper hole. "But I've definitely seen naked women before. I mean, not recently," he continued. *Just shut up already!* Hudson urged himself, but it was like his mouth was being controlled by a sadistic ventriloquist. "Apart from now that is. Not that you're completely naked yet."

"Yet?" said Tory, her eyebrow still as pointed as the needle in her hand.

Hudson winced. He was long past being able to salvage this encounter, and just wanted to skulk away like a scolded puppy. "I think I'll just go and come back when you're done," said Hudson, edging back towards the door. He was sure that if this continued for much longer, the heat of his skin would cause his hair to catch fire.

"Relax, Hudson Powell, I'm just messing with you," said Tory, pressing the needle through her skin again. "Are we clear of the moon?"

Hudson was relieved that Tory had steered the conversation onto less fleshy matters. He stepped back inside, but still tried not to look. Though the combination of her lack of clothing, plus the fact she was stitching herself up as casually as if she was repairing a ripped shirt, was hard to ignore. "Yes, we're clear, and I lost the RGF ships too. We're on course back to the portal now."

Tory finished stitching the wound, cut the thread with a pair of scissors, and placed the bloodied instruments into a surgical tray that was resting on the bed. She then stood up and stretched, before angling the side of her body towards Hudson. "How does it look?"

Hudson glanced down at the wound, noticing only then that it was one of three on Tory's side that she'd stitched up. The quality of the work was impressive, considering it was self-administered.

"You look great," said Hudson, before feeling another tug of embarrassment. "The stitching, I mean."

"What else would you be talking about?" asked Tory, folding her arms. This time she had raised both eyebrows at him.

Hudson's mouth fell open, but his brain had frozen. He had nothing. However, to his surprise, the next thing Tory did wasn't to punch him in the mouth, but smile.

"Are you normally this twitchy when you're alone with a woman?" asked Tory.

Hudson huffed a laugh, grateful that Tory had again relieved the tension between them, and also thankful that she hadn't hit him. "Not normally, no." Then he smiled back at her. "But then again, you're no ordinary woman, Tory Bellona."

Tory unfolded her arms, then grabbed Hudson's jacket. Before he knew what was happening, she'd pulled him towards her and kissed him. "That's for not leaving me behind."

Hudson's hands fell around Tory's waist. He tried to think of something poignant and heroic to say in response, but he didn't get the chance. Tory pulled him in close again, except this time it wasn't for a mere peck on the lips.

"Oh, shit, oh no!"

Hudson jerked away to see Liberty standing in the doorway of the medical bay. She had one hand over her eyes, and the other pressed to her hip; it was a perfect blend of stunned awkwardness. "I'm sorry, I should have knocked or something," she said. Despite the hand shielding her face, Hudson could see that she'd flushed a bright shade of crimson.

"That seems to be a common problem on this ship," said Tory. Though, unlike the mercenary's usual responses, it wasn't said in a snarky way.

Hudson watched, wide-eyed, as Tory grabbed her tank top from the bed, and pulled it on. She then threw her jacket over her shoulder, and said, "I'll see you two in the cockpit," before breezing out of the medical bay.

Hudson and Liberty remained in silence for a few seconds, before Liberty asked, "Is it over?" She was still shielding her face with her hand.

Hudson tutted, "Yes, 'it's over', you can look now."

Liberty lowered her hand, but she didn't meet Hudson's eyes, and was consciously trying to avoid even looking in his general direction. "Well, that was excruciating," she said.

"Speak for yourself..." said Hudson, smiling, but Liberty didn't appear to be amused. "What's up?" he added, giving Liberty an easy way out.

"I just came to tell you that Tobin is picking up some odd gravitational readings," Liberty said, finally managing to look Hudson in the eyes. "And I'm also picking up a crazy-high spike in Shaak radiation. I wanted to see what you made of it."

Hudson frowned, "A spike in Shaak radiation? Like when we opened a new portal?"

Liberty nodded, "Similar, but this is on a whole different scale. I'm talking at least an order of magnitude more intense."

Hudson took a deep breath and let it out slowly, before rubbing the back of his neck anxiously. Considering what he knew was coming, a large spike in Shaak radiation didn't sound like a good omen. He wished Morphus was on-hand to provide an explanation, but for now they were still on their own. "Then we'd better get back up there," replied Hudson, nodding towards the door.

Hudson followed Liberty back out through the living space and into the cockpit. Tory was standing behind the pilot's seat, looking more her usual, brooding self. Tobin noticed Hudson and Liberty come in, and slid out of the chair. He'd already spun the Orion around to face back towards the moon and gas giant, though the ship was still coasting towards the portal.

"The scanners are going crazy," said Tobin, as Hudson slipped in front of the controls. "I have no idea what to make of it."

Liberty dropped into the second seat, and Tobin moved up behind her. "The spatial distortions seem to be intensifying around the moon," said Liberty, checking the updated readings. She scowled at the new numbers as they flashed up on her monitor. "If I didn't know better, I'd say that a portal was opening, but it must be a hundred times the size of anything we've seen before."

"Look!" shouted Tobin, pointing out through the cockpit glass. A massive swirling vortex of purple energy was swelling in space, next to the moon. They all watched in stunned silence as it continued to grow, like a massive tropical cyclone being fed by warm ocean waters. Then there was a near-blinding flash, forcing Hudson to shield his eyes. However, when he opened them again, he couldn't believe what he saw. There was a ship emerging through the newly-created fold in space; but this was no ordinary vessel. In pure size alone, it made even the titanic Revocaters look ordinary. It was like an aged, battle-worn great white shark, that was scarred and hardened from countless victorious encounters with its prey.

"What the hell is that thing?" shrieked Tobin, his voice shaky and almost shrill.

"I don't know..." replied Liberty, her voice also frayed and uncertain.

However, Hudson knew exactly what it was. He'd seen it before, in his memories, at least. The memories that Morphus had implanted into his brain. The great ship had finally returned.

"That's Goliath," said Hudson, as calmly as he could manage. Then he met the eyes of each of the others in turn. "We have to go, right now. Because there's not a damn thing anyone or anything in this system can do to stop it."

CHAPTER 13

Hudson and the others stared on in awed silence as hundreds of smaller vessels seemed to eject from Goliath's surface. It was like watching a giant murmuration of starlings. Most flew down into the moon's atmosphere, while others darted towards the dozens of hunter ships fleeing the surface. Those that remained, swarmed around Goliath, forming a mesmerizing, constantly shifting dark cloud.

"What are those smaller vessels?" asked Liberty. "Are they like fighters or drones?"

"I've seen one of those things before," said Tory, unexpectedly speaking up. "We encountered one when we first entered the system. I don't know what they are, but we couldn't destroy it."

"Morphus called them seed ships," Hudson added, while checking the navigation scanner. Some of the alien vessels were accelerating rapidly towards the portal, pulling g-forces that no human being could withstand. Others were picking off the fleeing hunter ships, smashing through them like giant arrowheads. "They were originally designed to help Goliath spread life throughout the galaxy. Now they do the opposite."

"How do you know all this?" asked Tory.

"It's a long story, but I'll fill you in once we're safe," said Hudson, glancing up at her. Then he rotated the engine pods and began the deceleration burn for the portal transit. He checked the navigation scanner again, noting that the smaller alien vessels were still closing rapidly. "Assuming we make it to safety, that is. Those seed ships are coming in fast."

"How long until we reach the portal?" asked Tobin, his voice and posture still tense.

Hudson checked his readings again, "If I ignore all sensible safety precautions, and just charge straight for it, then three minutes, maybe four."

"And how long before those seed ships get here?" Tobin added, more hesitantly.

Hudson shrugged, and glanced back at Tobin. "I'm not going to lie, kid; we'll be cutting it pretty close."

Suddenly, an alarm rang out on Liberty's console, and all eyes turned to her. There were a breathless few seconds, before she finally spoke up. "I'm detecting another massive spike in Shaak radiation, even larger than before," said Liberty. "And it's coming from Goliath."

"Maybe it's leaving?" asked Tobin, but Hudson knew that was wishful thinking.

"No, it's..." said Liberty, but then she scowled at the data, hesitating.

"It's what, Liberty?" asked Hudson, practically on the edge of his seat.

"These readings don't make any sense," replied Liberty, tapping angrily at her keypad. "It's like there's another portal opening, but the co-ordinates can't be right. They put it in the center of the moon."

"There's a portal opening in the center of the moon?" replied Hudson. However, repeating what Liberty had said didn't cause it to make any more sense.

"That's what the readings say," said Liberty, still doubtful. "I can't explain it."

Hudson glanced back out of the cockpit glass at the great ship. It had now angled its nose towards the planet, as if it were a predator preparing to pounce. Suddenly, there was another massive flash of purple light, and a giant portal vortex began to grow. It was forming on the opposite side of the moon to where Goliath was looming.

"There's something emerging from the new vortex," said Liberty, her voice tense and jittery.

"Is it another ship?" asked Hudson, but Liberty shook her head.

"I'm detecting metals, but no power signatures," said Liberty, now sounding more confused than anxious. "Superheated iron and nickel, plus some other elements I can't identify." Then her brow furrowed even more deeply, before she turned to Hudson, wearing a look of pure astonishment. "It's the moon's core! Goliath has created a portal between the moon's center and that new vortex. It's like the portal swallowed the moon's entire core, and spat it out into space!"

"How is that even possible?" said Hudson, "Goliath's crystal was destroyed; it shouldn't be able to create portals."

Liberty shrugged, "I don't know. It shouldn't be able to core a moon like it was an apple, either, but that's what it just did."

Liberty's console chimed an alert again. She read the data, shaking her head in disbelief the whole time. She turned to the others, her face suddenly pale, and said, "The moon is collapsing..."

Hudson was again about to parrot what Liberty had said, as if repeating her words would somehow provide a different answer. However, he was suddenly rapt by the scene unfolding in front of him. With the moon's inner core vanishing through a fold in space, the outer core had violently collapsed into the void left behind. This had caused the surface of the moon to crack, like a tray of toffee smashed with a hammer. It was an event of such cataclysmic intensity that the moon had begun to rip itself apart.

Hudson was unable to tear his eyes away, but the worst and most horrific scenes were still to come. The ejected metallic core had been expelled close enough to the moon to be trapped by its gravity. It then plummeted into the surface, like an enormous wrecking ball. The resulting impact smashed the moon into pieces.

Goliath had remained still, silently observing the carnage from its perch. Then as the moon broke apart, the great ship began to turn. It angled its nose in the direction of the portal leading to Sapphire Alpha, and slowly began to advance.

"I think it's time we left," said Tory Bellona. Considering what they'd all just seen, her voice was remarkably composed.

"I think you're right..." Hudson answered, with considerably less poise. He grabbed the controls, and spun the Orion away from the carnage behind them. He saw that their deceleration burn had completed, but the enormity of the events that had just unfolded had caused him to take his eyes off the navigation scanner. There were six seed ships directly on their tail, the portal was still a minute away, and there was now also a fleet of ten RGF Patrol Craft heading straight for them.

"I sure hope those cops are gunning for the seed ships, and not us," said Tobin, who was now gripping the back of Liberty's seat tightly.

"You'd hope so, but with the RGF you never can tell," replied Hudson. Then he glanced back at Tobin and Tory. "I'd sit down and strap in, this might get a little sporty."

Tory activated the second auxiliary seat and Hudson heard the harnesses click into place behind him. He then adjusted his grip on the controls and took a deep breath. He was about to play chicken with ten RGF patrol craft, but there was no question of him backing down first. He knew the seed ships were even deadlier than a fleet of armed RGF vessels.

Hudson glanced at the scanner and noted that the first of the seed ships was about to overtake them, but none of the alien vessels appeared to be targeting the Orion. Suddenly, two of the black arrowheads raced past the cockpit window and ripped straight through three RGF Patrol Craft, as easily as if they were egg crates.

"Hang on!" cried Hudson, as he veered hard to avoid the fiery debris. The seed ships banked and turned back towards them, displaying impossible agility. Another two RGF patrol craft were pulverized. Debris showered the cockpit, rattling off the glass like hailstones. Hudson banked hard again, setting them back on course for the portal, and pushed the throttle forward.

"You can't transit at this speed!" yelled Tobin, "The stress could tear us apart."

Hudson held his course, "Those damn seed ships will smash us to pieces if I don't!" he yelled back. "We don't have a choice."

The navigation scanner flashed a warning, and Hudson checked it quickly, seeing that a seed ship was now on their tail. He noted the distance to the portal, and pushed the throttle a notch further forward. "Clench up, people, this is going to be rough!" he called out.

The seed ship veered in, but Hudson pulsed the thrusters just in time, rotating the Orion in a desperate attempt to avoid a collision. Alarms rang out as the alien ship clipped their starboard wing, sending the Orion into a spin. Screams and cries filled the cockpit as they tumbled towards the portal, completely out of control. Hudson could see that several damage warning lights had lit up on his panel, likely from the impact with the seed ship. Yet, incredibly, they were still intact, and still breathing. Hudson silently thanked Morphus' retrofitted alien enhancements for saving their skins.

"Ten seconds!" yelled Hudson, though his cries were lost in the chaos of other shouts. The controls had become unresponsive, so that even if Hudson wanted to stop their transit, he couldn't. All they could do now was wait, and roll the dice.

The Orion continued to hurtle towards the portal, tumbling chaotically, end-over-end. Then they hit the threshold hard, like a diver belly-flopping into a swimming pool. They were all jolted brutally, then the cockpit was consumed by purple light. The vortex outside swirled around them like a storm, as they tumbled through the fold in space.

Hudson could hear the hull of the ship creak and groan under the immense pressures. Any ordinary ship would have been torn apart from the stress, but the Orion was no ordinary VCX-110. Infused with alien DNA, Hudson knew it could take the strain. Or, at least he hoped it could - because they had to survive. The great ship, Goliath, was coming for Earth, and he had to stop it.

CHAPTER 14

The Orion emerged on the Sapphire-Alpha side of the portal, still tumbling out of control. Hudson's instruments were all down, and warning lights and indicators were flashing across every console. Yet, despite their uncontrolled spin, he could still use the one instrument that was working – his eyes. Through the cockpit glass, he could see the imposing outlines of three Martian heavy cruisers. And the Orion was heading straight for them, like a cannonball.

"You need to level us off," Liberty cried out. "The main drives will be down; I need to get to the engine room!"

Hudson wrestled with the controls, pulsing the thrusters in a desperate attempt to rectify their spin, but the ship wasn't responding. "The drives are still online," he shouted back to Liberty, "but the flight controls are not answering and the main computer is offline. You have to reinitialize the system!"

"How can the drive systems still be online?" Liberty called back. "We just transitioned through a portal!"

"How about we talk about that some other time?" Hudson answered, trying to focus Liberty on more pressing matters. His eyes grew wide as the heavy cruisers began to dominate the view outside. The MP ships were already taking evasive action, but they were slow and cumbersome. Unless Hudson could regain control, the Orion would smash straight into them. Or, more likely, Hudson realized, be blasted into dust before that happened. "You have to get the flight systems back online, or we're dead!"

Liberty sprang into action, pulling open the primary service panel and practically diving inside. Anxious seconds slipped by, with every tick of the clock bringing them closer to destruction. "Any time now, Liberty!" Hudson cried out, as the turrets on the MP ships began to draw down on them.

"Damn it, the main power breaker is fried," Liberty answered, poking her head back out of the panel, "I need to replace it."

"There's no time," cried Hudson, "We have five or ten seconds before they start shooting!"

Suddenly, Tory unclipped her harness and practically fell to Liberty's side, before pulling a knife from her boot. "Get back," she cried.

Liberty immediately pulled her head out of the compartment and grabbed her chair to steady herself. "What are you going to do?" she said, staring at the metal blade glinting in Tory's hand. A few days ago, Hudson would have half-expected Tory to plunge it into Liberty's gut, but instead, she thrust it inside the compartment.

"Something that I hope works," Tory answered, through gritted teeth. Levering the damaged breaker out of its housing, she then rammed the blade between the contacts. There was a loud crack and a flash of light, and Tory was sent hurtling backwards.

"Tory!" cried Hudson, seeing the mercenary laid out on the deck, smoke rising from her body. He reached for the buckle to release his harness, but then the flight deck suddenly kicked back into life. He was desperate to check on Tory, but if he didn't maneuver the ship to safety, she was dead anyway.

"I'll go!" shouted Liberty, scrambling to Tory's side.

Hudson forced himself to look away, grabbing the controls again. This time the thrusters and main engines responded. Flying on gut feeling alone, he tried to counteract the Orion's spin, pulsing the thrusters little and often. Soon he'd leveled off the ship, but they were still careering towards an MP cruiser. An alarm rang out, and Hudson glanced at his panel. "Target lock, they're firing!" he shouted, before spinning the ship away from the cruiser and pushing the throttle hard forward. "Hang on!"

The kick of the engines was brutal, but the sudden change in velocity was enough to push them away from the cruiser. Hudson had no idea if the MP ship had fired and missed, but he had no intention of giving them another opportunity to blow them away. He grabbed his headset and pulled it on, before opening a channel on the distress frequency.

"MP cruiser, MP cruiser, do not fire!" he yelled into the mic. "I have regained control. I say again, do not fire!"

Hudson throttled back and then spun the engine pods around to kill their forward momentum. He watched as the three MP Heavy Cruisers returned to their previous formation. The open channel crackled with static, until the lead cruiser finally responded.

"VCX-110 K2000-Shadow, this is MP Heavy Cruiser Acheron," a voice replied on the open channel. "Hold your position and prepare to be boarded."

"Prepare to be boarded?" Hudson repeated, "For what reason?"

"You are under arrest, by the command of Admiral Shelby. The charges are illegal ID registry reprogramming and collusion with enemy agents. Do not attempt to run, or you will be fired upon."

"Shelby again..." said Hudson, shaking his head. "We just can't seem to catch a break at the moment."

Suddenly, another voice crackled over the speaker. "MP Cruiser Acheron, this is Commodore Trent of the Coalition of Earth Territories." Hudson checked the navigation scanner, which had finished reinitializing, and saw that three more ships were rapidly closing in. Their IDs read as CET Super Frigates – more than a match for the MP cruisers. "We also wish to speak with Captain Powell. I suggest a rendezvous and parlay at Rapture Base, on Sapphire Alpha."

Silence filled the cabin of the Orion, punctuated only by the occasional crackle and hiss of the open communications channel.

"Commodore Trent, this is Admiral Shelby," came the stern female voice, which Hudson immediately recognized. "You have no jurisdiction here. Powell is wanted by the MP military for crimes committed in MP space. This is none of your concern."

"Admiral, you have no jurisdiction here either," Trent replied, smoothly. "So, unless you intend for our two fleets to fight it out over who gets custody of Captain Powell, I suggest we pursue a more equitable course of action."

There was another anxious wait, before Shelby eventually answered. "Very well, I agree to meet at Rapture Base," she said, sounding vexed. Then in the haughty manner that typified the MP military, Shelby added, "But if Powell attempts to run, or you attempt to take custody of him first, we will see whose fleet is the more powerful."

The channel went dead. Hudson threw down the headset and slumped back in his chair, letting out a long, exasperated sigh. Then he remembered about Tory being shocked and thrown back, and he spun around, his heart racing. Tory was sitting up, aided by Liberty, and was rubbing the back of her head. Her right hand was badly burned, and she was clearly in pain, but Tory did not appear concerned.

"I'm beginning to think I was safer back on that shitty little moon," she said dryly, standing up and cradling her injured hand in front of her body.

Tobin laughed, then noticed that no-one else was joining in. "What? That was pretty funny!" he said, frowning at the others.

Tory glowered at him, and raised her burned hand in front of his face. "Do you find this amusing?" she said, fixing him with an icy stare.

The blood flushed from Tobin's cheeks, and he just stammered a response, "Erm... well... no?"

"Good," replied Tory. Then she turned to Hudson, and said, "I'll be in the medical bay.

Again." She opened the door and walked through it, without another word.

Hudson got up and threw his arm around Tobin, who was still looking shell-shocked. "Pro-tip number two, kid..." he said, in a mentorlike manner. "Tory Bellona doesn't do jokes..."

CHAPTER 15

Rapture Base was the name of the scavenger town on the surface of Sapphire Alpha. Like most scavenger towns in the outer portal worlds, it was a treacherous, ramshackle place that any sane person consciously avoided. However, the wreck on the surface of the planet still attracted enough hunters to ensure the various seedy establishments saw plenty of trade.

The arrival of six powerful military cruisers in orbit would normally be enough to spook most hunters into fleeing the surface. Though as Hudson descended towards their designated meeting spot, on a plain a kilometer outside the town's borders, he realized that most had already fled. News of the alien attack and the destruction of the moon had already begun to spread like wildfire. Very soon it would be all over the wire services and epapers; then, there would be panic.

Hudson set the Orion down, then opened the rear cargo ramp. The MP and CET cruisers were all too large to land, but Hudson could see two shuttles approaching – one from each lead ship. Both shuttles had two accompanying patrol craft escorts. To Hudson this seemed like an excessive and unnecessary precaution, considering most of the hunters had already left. However, it served to highlight the deep level of mistrust between Shelby and Trent.

Hudson shut down the engines then met the others outside. Sapphire Alpha was a lush, green world, but it was late autumn on the continent where they had landed. The skies were blanketed with swirling gray clouds, and the air was wet and cold. It was a suitably miserable setting for what would inevitably be a gloomy discussion.

"How do we play this?" asked Liberty, as the two shuttles set down a hundred meters apart. The escort ships continued to circle above the meeting site. "I mean, how much do we tell them?"

Hudson sucked in a lungful of the chilly air and let it out with a shrug. "I really don't think there's any point in holding back now," he said, watching Shelby and Trent start to walk towards them. Each of them had two armed guards. "They'll know what just happened, and I already told Trent about Morphus. Hopefully, now they can trust their own eyes too."

"And what about Cutler and Griff?" Liberty added. This perked the interest of Tory, who was now paying close attention to the conversation.

"We tell them that they have the crystal," said Hudson. "We tell them it's imperative we get it back, and why. Hell, we could really use their help to find those assholes."

"They won't be able to find Cutler," interrupted Tory, as she observed the two military parties approaching. "But I can."

Tory's interjections remained as intriguing as ever, but Hudson didn't get a chance to dig deeper before Shelby and Trent arrived.

"Hudson Powell and Liberty Devan," said Commodore Trent, nodding respectfully to each in turn. "It's good to see you again. Much has happened since our last encounter, as I'm sure you are both aware."

"You can say that again," replied Hudson, shaking the hand that Trent offered him.

"I see that your troop has expanded," Trent continued, smiling at Tobin and then Tory.

"Tobin Rand," said Tobin, brightly, extending a hand to Trent, who accepted it, gladly.

"Ah, young Master Rand, I know your mother," said Trent. Hudson noticed that Liberty and Admiral Shelby both rolled their eyes in almost perfect unison.

"Why does that not surprise me?" replied Tobin, though he was still smiling.

Then with considerably more reticence, Trent offered his hand to Tory. "And you are?"

Tory rested her thumbs through her gun belt, "Someone who you should stop talking to," she replied, coolly. Hudson could see Trent's two guards tense up as Tory's freshly-bandaged hand approached her holstered revolver.

Trent nodded, and withdrew his outstretched hand. "As you wish," he said, though his manner was still pleasant and diplomatic.

"Are you quite finished with the pointless and unnecessary introductions now?" Shelby cut in, rudely. Her expression was almost the exact opposite of Trent's gregarious openness. "And, in case you were interested, the ill-mannered mercenary is Tory Bellona," Shelby added, pointing to Tory. Shelby seemed to enjoy the fact she knew something that Trent did not. "The number of crimes and misdemeanors that she is connected with would fill an entire data pad twice over."

"Such a shame you can't prove any of it," said Tory, shooting Shelby a provoking smile.

Shelby glowered back at Tory, but Trent was quick to steer the subject of the discussion back on topic. "I think the current situation is more serious than a single mercenary's petty misdemeanors," said Trent, turning to Shelby. "And it is much larger than this one ship and crew."

Shelby took a step forward, "I disagree," she said, before aiming a perfectly manicured finger at Hudson. "Captain Powell was seen accompanying a hostile alien vessel, and refused commands to stop. Now we have another alien vessel at our borders; one that wields unimaginable power. And Powell is again at the center of events. He has much to explain, and I intend to get answers."

Hudson held up his hands, trying to placate a clearly incensed Admiral Shelby. "Look, I'll explain everything, or at least what I can," he began. "But it's going to require a leap of faith on your part, because what I have to say is going to sound crazy."

"Admiral, if I may," Trent interjected, clearly eager to get Shelby on-side. "We have an alien vessel the size of a city advancing on the core systems. And our reports confirm that it is capable of destroying entire planets. I think very little faith is required at this point."

"Speak for yourself, Commodore," Shelby cut-in. "There is no confirmed evidence that this vessel was responsible for the destruction of the moon."

This time it was Trent who held up a hand in an attempt to calm the inflaming tensions. "Look, Admiral, the specific details are unimportant right now," he said. "I think we can all agree that this alien vessel is a threat, and that it's in our shared interests to work together?" He waited to see how

Shelby reacted to this suggestion. The Admiral simply folded her arms, and nodded, allowing Trent to continue. The Commodore turned back to Hudson, and said, "Now, what can you tell us, Captain Powell?"

Hudson spent the next few minutes detailing the story of how he and Liberty came across the crystal, and later, the alien AI, Morphus. He explained to an open-minded Trent, but still heavily skeptical Shelby, how Morphus had implanted memories into his brain. He detailed the history of the race Morphus called the Corporeals, and their role in spreading life throughout the galaxy, including to Earth. And he revealed how the crystal was the only weapon that could defeat Goliath, and how it had been stolen by Cutler Wendell and Logan Griff. Both senior military commanders listened without interruptions, but while Trent was introspective, Hudson could see that Shelby's frustrations were deepening.

"Do you really expect me to believe this outrageous fantasy story?" snapped Shelby, after Hudson had finished. "A ship called 'Goliath', a shape-shifting artificial intelligence, and god-like beings called 'Corporeals'? It's preposterous!"

Trent again stepped in to offer his arguments, but Hudson could sense that the Commodore was not going to turn Shelby to his opinion. "Admiral, for the last century, we have discovered dozens of alien worlds through engineered worm-holes, and raided crashed alien vessels for their technology," Trent said, in his measured, reasonable tone. "Clearly, these alien artefacts pre-dated human life on Earth. And the portals and alien hulks must have been created by someone, or something. We all just stopped asking who built them, and why. So, is it really so much of a stretch to believe Captain Powell's story?"

Shelby waved her hand dismissively, "A story is all this is," she said. "Where is this Morphus thing now? If it is real, why does it not reveal itself?"

Hudson shrugged, "Look, Admiral, all I've told you is the truth. It's up to you whether you believe me or not." Then he pointed up into the sky, and added, "But Goliath is coming. And without that crystal, nothing will stand in its way."

Shelby straightened up, as if Hudson had directly challenged her. "We shall see about that, Captain Powell," she said, with a healthy measure of pomposity. "If this 'Goliath' dares to enter Martian space, my armada shall make short work of it." Then she turned to leave.

"Admiral, at least put out a warrant for Cutler Wendell's vessel, FS-31 Patrol Craft Hawk 1333F," Trent called out after her. Shelby halted and turned to listen. "You may not believe that the crystal has significance, but what would it hurt to have it in our possession? Besides, it will prevent these miscreants from opening any other portals."

"Fine," said Shelby. "I shall issue the warrant, if only to ensure no further portals are found. But I remain doubtful that this crystal Captain Powell talks about has any importance. The might of the MP Armada will be sufficient to crush this threat." Then she aimed her finger at Trent, "I suggest you also assemble your forces, Commodore. Trust in what you know, not this fairytale nonsense about crystals and alien artificial beings."

Then Shelby spun on her heels and began marching back to her ship. Her guard escorts waited for the Admiral to pass between them, before turnning and marching after her.

Commodore Trent let out an exasperated sigh, and then turned to Hudson. "Martians..." he said, with a knowing smile.

Hudson laughed and returned the smile. "Martians..." he repeated, before becoming more earnest. "But thanks for handling Shelby. If you hadn't shown up, I think I'd be in a Martian holding cell by now."

Trent acknowledged the thank you with a courteous nod. "You're welcome, Captain. Though I suggest that you still give the esteemed Admiral a wide berth from now on."

"Honestly, I hope I never see her again," replied Hudson. "But somehow, I doubt I'll be so lucky."

One of Trent's armed guards walked up to the Commodore and spoke quietly into his ear. Trent nodded, and turned back to Hudson. "I'm afraid I must leave now," he began. "But I will put out the arrest warrant for Cutler Wendell and Logan Griff at once. And I will feed any intelligence relating to his whereabouts directly to you."

"You won't find him," interrupted Tory. "Cutler has been evading you people all his life. Now is no different." She turned to Hudson, before adding, "We're wasting time here. I'll wait for you on the ship." Then she left the group, and began walking back towards the Orion.

Trent smiled again, "The formidable Tory Bellona certainly lives up to her reputation," he said, after the mercenary had passed out of earshot.

"I thought you didn't know who she was?" replied Hudson, with a curious frown.

"Her alleged list of crimes and misdemeanors is not limited merely to MP worlds," Trent replied, with a twinkle in his eyes. "Stay in touch, Captain Powell. I will assemble my fleet at Earth, but if this Morphus returns, and needs help, the CET military is at your disposal."

"Thanks, it's nice to have an ally for a change," said Hudson. Then they shook hands, and Trent also departed. Hudson, Liberty and Tobin watched the two shuttles lift off, then turned back to the Orion.

"So, what do we do now?" asked Liberty, pulling her jacket tighter to cut out the cold wind.

"We find Cutler, and get the crystal back," said Hudson. "And I have a feeling that Tory knows where to find him."

They reached the foot of the Orion's cargo ramp, ducking into the wind and bracing against the cold, as the bitter currents whipped past them.

"I wish that Morphus was here," said Liberty. "We could really use its help right now."

They all started up the ramp, but then froze. Standing at the top was Morphus, in the same female form that Hudson had last seen her in. And next to it, aiming her revolver at its head, was Tory Bellona.

"Greetings again, Liberty Devan entity. I am pleased to see that you are still functioning," said Morphus.

Liberty was too stunned to speak, but Hudson was quick to act. "Tory, it's okay, put the gun down. This is a friend!"

Tory scowled. "You know this woman?" she said, and Hudson was sure he detected a hint of jealousy in her voice. "Who is she?"

"It's not a she," said Hudson. "This is Morphus."

Morphus turned to Tory, and suddenly transformed, adopting an exact likeness of Hudson Powell. "Based on your emotional reaction, body language and pheromone responses, I have determined that this form is more pleasing to you," said Morphus. Tory's mouth fell open. "Am I correct?"

Now it was Hudson who was lost for words. Luckily, Morphus' sudden transformation seemed to have neutralized Tory's natural belligerence. She decocked and holstered her weapon, before folding her arms. She looked first at Morphus, then at Hudson. "I think I was definitely safer back on that moon..."

CHAPTER 16

The party reconvened in the living space of the Orion. Morphus, Tobin and Liberty had squeezed onto the semi-circular couch, while Tory stood just off to the side. She looked ill-at-ease. Despite her redemption in the eyes of Liberty, she was still amongst people who were recently enemies, and it showed in her rigid posture. Hudson realized that Tory didn't yet feel that she belonged, and maybe she never would do. Trust was something that was hard to accept when you'd lived an entire life without it.

Hudson went to the cabinet beside the couch and set a bottle of Ma's whiskey and five tumblers on the table. He then poured healthy measures of the powerful liquor into each glass.

Tobin scowled at the ominous square bottle, and then looked up at Hudson, "I don't suppose you have any wine?"

Hudson looked at him like he'd asked for a glass of engine oil, "You don't suppose correctly, kid."

Tobin shrugged, "Oh well, Goliath is going to kill us all, anyway," he said, before picking up the tumbler, "so I guess it doesn't matter if this takes me out first."

Hudson smiled, and raised his own glass, "That's the spirit."

They each drank from the tumblers, except Morphus, who simply waited for them to finish. The mood around the table was as dark as the joke that Tobin had just told. With time to reflect on what had happened at the new portal world, the true enormity of events was hitting them all. Even Tory seemed subdued.

"I'm glad to see that you're all healed up and repaired," Hudson said to Morphus, placing his empty tumbler on the table. "But I'm afraid things have taken a turn for the worse while you were gone. We're all hoping you have some good news."

"Have you managed to reacquire the crystal?" asked Morphus, somewhat evasively. The alien AI had since transformed back into the female form Hudson was familiar with, rather than appearing as his doppelgänger.

Hudson shrugged, "I'm afraid not. We tracked Cutler and Griff to the moon through the newly-opened portal, but they escaped. Then Goliath showed up, and all hell broke loose."

Morphus cocked its head to the side, thoughtfully. "Then I do not have any good news right now. The return of the crystal is imperative."

Liberty took a sip of her whiskey and then cut in. "Speaking of crystals, how was Goliath able to create a portal?" she asked. "I thought its crystal had been destroyed after you banished it?"

Morphus now cocked its head to the other side, before answering. "During its voyage, the great ship had collected crystal fragments from fallen Revocaters. Before your crystal was activated, Goliath was lost, and blind to the locations of any portals. But your crystal lit a path back to System 5118208. Along the way, it not only collected its seed ships, but the resources needed to recombine a crystal also."

Hudson sighed and poured himself another measure, before topping up the other glasses. "If that's true, we don't stand a chance. That ship just destroyed an entire moon as if it were popping a balloon."

"A creative analogy," said Morphus, narrowing its eyes at Hudson. "Though also inaccurate. The moon collapsed inward due to the instantaneous removal of millions of tons of core matter. A balloon is filled with gas, and pops due to its surface structure being punctured, and the high-pressure gas rapidly escaping."

Hudson scowled, "I think you get my point though."

"I do," said Morphus, calmly. "To continue your creatively-inaccurate balloon analogy, Goliath is now venting its rage. For many thousands of years, it has been denied its purpose. For many thousands of years, it has lived with its failure, growing ever more bitter and resentful. It is no longer satisfied with the extermination of sentient corporeal life. It will obliterate all of the planets that humans now inhabit, down to the very last. It will save Earth until the end. Its destruction will be Goliath's crowning glory."

A deathly silence fell over the room. Morphus' monologue had hit them all like a sledgehammer. Hudson had already felt mentally battered before he'd entered the living space, but Trent's support had buoyed him a little. Now, he was consumed by utter hopelessness.

"What was your good news?" asked Tory, who was the only one not staring down into the bottom of an empty tumbler. "You said you don't have any good news, 'right now'. That suggests there is the potential for some, right?"

Hudson hadn't picked up on that particular detail at the time, but Tory was right. And Morphus was nothing if not exacting; it wouldn't have phrased it in that way without reason.

Morphus nodded at Tory, "You are correct, Tory Bellona entity," it said. "At the Corporeals' homeworld, I was not only able to repair my damaged systems, but also interface with the

Telescope. It showed me Goliath, and something more."

Hudson was hanging off the alien AI's every word, and from the looks on the faces of the others, they were enthralled too.

"The possible good news," Morphus continued, "is that I have also discovered a sole surviving Revocater."

"You mean the ships like the hulks that are smashed on the surfaces of the portal worlds?" asked Liberty.

Morphus nodded again, "Correct. It is the prototype on which all the others were modeled."

"And it's still intact?" said Hudson, feeling a tingle of excitement energize his weary muscles.

"It is intact, yes," replied Morphus.

"And it's operational?" Hudson added, becoming increasingly annoyed at having to coax every last bit of information out of the alien. "You can fly it?"

"It lacks a crystal, but otherwise yes," Morphus replied.

Hudson laughed and threw his arms out wide. "Well, shit, Morphus; that sounds like pretty good news to me!"

Morphus frowned at Hudson's excitable reaction, but his enthusiasm was catching. The previously stony expressions on the faces of Tobin and Liberty had also lifted.

"So, what's the catch, lady?" asked Tory. She had been the only one not to show any excitement at

Morphus' news, almost to the point of aloofness. "There's a catch, right?"

Hudson lowered his arms and hugged his shoulders, anxiously waiting for Morphus to answer. He was almost angry at Tory for trying to find more problems. However, even from the limited range of expressions that Morphus displayed, it was clear that Tory had guessed correctly.

"There is a complication," Morphus confirmed, and Hudson felt his mouth go dry. "The prototype Revocater differs from the others in a number of respects, but one in particular is key," it continued. "It requires two pilots."

Hudson sighed and rubbed the back of his neck. His muscles were suddenly weary again. "And I don't suppose there's another Morphus out there anywhere to help you fly it?" he asked.

"There is not," replied Morphus. "I am the last of my kind."

"I'm still waiting for the but..." added Hudson, hopefully.

"But..." said Morphus, causing Hudson to perk up. "...there is an alternative. I can operate the Revocater's core systems, and effectively function as its brain. But in so doing, I will be unable to pilot the vessel."

"Okay, so then I can be your pilot, right?" suggested Hudson. "I've flown every kind of ship you can think of; how hard can it be to fly a Revocater?"

"Your enthusiasm is endearing, Hudson Powell," replied Morphus, "but your corporeal flying skills are irrelevant. The pilot must be augmented, in order to interface with the Revocater. Any skills that are required, I can implant directly into the subject's brain."

"Whoa, wait a minute," interrupted Liberty. "Augmented how? Like some sort of cyborg?"

Morphus seemed to think for a moment, but then smiled and nodded back at Liberty. "Yes, like some sort of cyborg." It glanced up at Hudson, and added, "That was an example of an accurate analogy." Hudson scowled, but Morphus simply continued, unaware of the embarrassment it had caused. "The augmentations will bond elements of my material structure and technology directly into your musculoskeletal structure and brain."

Liberty's eyes widened. She quickly grabbed her drink and threw down the contents in one. She then slammed the glass down, and said, "Hard pass, thanks."

Hudson laughed, "Don't worry, Liberty. If this is what it takes then I'll do it."

"I'm afraid the augmentation requires a specific level of neural efficiency. Your brain lacks the necessary sophistication," said Morphus. The lack of feeling in its delivery made the sentence come across as cold and insulting.

Liberty sniggered and raised her empty glass at Hudson, "Morphus means that your cyborg IQ isn't high enough."

Hudson felt like flipping Liberty the middle finger, but managed to restrain himself.

"What about me?" asked Tobin, who had been largely silent. However, he'd also finished his whiskey, which Hudson figured had probably emboldened him. "How's my brain?"

"Also unsuitable," said Morphus.

Tobin didn't look particularly disappointed at the answer, and was curiously also smiling. "What's so amusing about having an 'unsuitable brain'?" Hudson asked.

"It's better than an unsophisticated one," Tobin answered, still smiling. Liberty sniggered again.

Morphus then looked at Tory, but she quickly held up a finger to stop it before it spoke. "Before you say anything, I don't care if my brain is suitable, unsuitable, or anywhere in-between," she said. "And it sure as hell isn't sophisticated. But there's no way you're augmenting *me*, lady."

Morphus nodded, "As you wish. Though, as it turns out, I have already determined a compatible match."

"Oh, no you don't," said Liberty, also wagging a finger at the alien.

"The Liberty Devan entity has a seventy-six percent chance of a successful augmentation," Morphus continued, ignoring Liberty's protests.

"Or a twenty-four percent chance of you turning my brain to mashed potato!" Liberty exclaimed. "No thanks, there has to be another way."

"There is not," said Morphus. "None that doesn't risk significant delay and the inevitable destruction of the entire human race."

Liberty snorted and shook her head, "Great... Well, when you put it like that."

There was another tomblike silence in the room. Morphus had offered them a lifeline, but it was not without risk. And Hudson was acutely aware that Liberty had only just escaped from the jaws of death.

"What risk is there to Liberty if this doesn't work?" asked Hudson, skipping ahead slightly. "Can you offer any assurances that she'll be safe?"

"I cannot," said Morphus, again with a clinical coolness. The entity was merely serving up the facts, uncolored by emotion. As much as this sounded harsh, Hudson realized it was better than being deceived, intentionally or otherwise.

He looked at Liberty and Liberty met his eyes. He knew what she was going to do, and as much as he wanted to stop her, he knew he wouldn't be able to. However, what was even more difficult to accept was that he knew he shouldn't even try. Too much was at stake to play it safe now.

"It seems I don't have a choice," said Liberty, pouring herself another drink.

"You always have a choice, Liberty Devan," said Morphus, but Liberty shook her head.

"The choice is that I either do this, or Goliath kills everyone, right?" Morphus nodded. "Then there's no choice. I'll do it."

"Very well," replied Morphus. "I will return to my ship and prepare the procedure." Then Morphus turned to Hudson. "However, even with two pilots, the Revocater will be useless against Goliath without the crystal."

"I'll get it," said Hudson, with a renewed determination. Their situation was still precarious, but it was no longer hopeless. "I don't know how yet, but I'll get it."

"You'll need me," said Tory. "I can find Cutler Wendell. And besides, we have a score to settle."

Hudson nodded, "Thanks. It looks like I need someone new in the second seat, anyway."

Tory scoffed a laugh, "Like hell... I've seen your flying. The second seat is yours."

Hudson was about to object when Tobin spoke up. "What about me? I still want to help, and there's no way I'm going back to Mars. My mom would kill me!"

Liberty laughed, but it was not meant unkindly. "Maybe you could come with me?" she said, glancing across to Morphus to check its reaction. "I have a feeling I could use the support."

Morphus nodded. "Piloting the Revocater will result in significant physical and mental strain," it said, seemingly agreeing with Liberty's suggestion. "There will be times when the stresses become difficult to bear. A companion for what I believe you call, 'moral support', may be advantageous."

Liberty winced, "You're not really selling this to me, Morphus."

The alien frowned, but Tobin smiled and cut-in, "Don't worry, I'll have your back."

Hudson went around the table, refilling everyone's glasses. "For what it's worth, it sounds like we have a plan." He picked up his glass, and offered a toast. "Here's to kicking Goliath's ass."

They all drank, including to Hudson's surprise, Morphus. The alien placed the glass down on the table, and examined the remaining contents inquisitively. "This liquid is similar to the one I sampled previously. Its alcohol content remains highly toxic to human beings," it announced. "In addition to numerous deleterious consequences, it will increase your arousal and excitement, lower inhibitions and increase impulsivity."

Tory grabbed the square bottle off the table, and held it up to Morphus. "That's the whole damn point of it, lady," she said, before placing the neck to her lips and taking a long gulp. Then she looked at Hudson, and said, "I'll get started on the checklist. Let me know when you're ready to leave." Then she swept off towards the cockpit, bottle still in hand.

CHAPTER 17

A ripple of tracer rounds flashed past the cockpit of the FS-31, as the red planet loomed large ahead of them. "Shit, they're really serious about us powering down," said Logan Griff, arching his neck to get a better view aft. The two MP patrol vessels were still on their tail. "Why the hell did you bring us to Mars if this ship is on a damned MP watch list?"

"It's not," replied Cutler, coolly. "Or, at least it wasn't."

A priority communication channel clicked opened and the haughty voice of an MP officer filled the cockpit. "FS-31 Patrol Craft Hawk 1333F, you are under arrest by order of Admiral Shelby," the officer began. His voice was thick with self-importance. "Power down immediately, or you will be fired upon."

As if to reinforce his point, the lead Martian patrol ship fired again, sending another volley of tracer rounds past their nose. The shots flew by so close that Griff instinctively ducked away from them. "Cutler, these assholes aren't messing around, we have to abort and find somewhere else to dock." Cutler didn't answer, and Griff realized that he was still holding course towards the planet, and that his approach velocity was dangerously high. "What are you doing?" he demanded, growing suddenly even more nervous of Cutler's intentions than those of the high-and-mighty MP officer. "You keep going like this, and we'll just burn up in the Martian atmosphere!"

"This is the only way to escape the patrol," replied Cutler, while making several rapid adjustments to his flight controls. His voice was still calm, and he did not deviate from his course. "I will need you to stand ready to jump-start the main drives on my command."

"What the hell are you going to do?" cried Griff, as the entry-warning indicators flashed up on his panel, followed by a low, strident alarm.

"If you want to survive, just do as I say," snapped Cutler. "There's no time to explain."

Griff growled in reply, before pulling the engineering panel closer to his seat. He accessed the reactor and main drive controls, then waited. He was again a powerless spectator, at the mercy of whatever plan Cutler Wendell had devised.

The ship rocked and shimmied as it hit turbulence in the exosphere, but still Cutler didn't deviate or slow down. The mercenary was watching his instruments with an almost trance-like focus. He then dove towards the planet more steeply and flames engulfed the view outside. Alarms rang out again, louder and more urgent than before.

"Too fast!" Griff yelled out, but he couldn't hear his own voice over the din in the cockpit. He tried to cry out again, but although his mouth opened, and he could feel the vibrations shake his chest, his ears were deaf to any sounds he made.

Suddenly, the FS-31 emerged through the inferno, and Cutler yanked back on the controls to pull the nose up. There was a powerful jolt as the main drives kicked in, leveling them off. Then Griff saw the drive systems go offline on his panel, and he panicked. "They've hit the engines! They're offline, we have to bail out!" he cried.

"I disabled the drives," answered Cutler, his own voice now escalating as the shimmies through the deck plating intensified. "They're targeting our drive signature. This will make us harder to hit."

Griff stared at Cutler in disbelief; entering the Martian atmosphere without the main drives was suicide. However, he didn't get an opportunity to protest, because suddenly the pressure in the cabin dropped sharply and another alarm rang out.

"Hull breach!" cried Cutler, veering hard to port using the thrusters. "Find it and seal it!"

Air rushed past Griff's face as he craned his neck around the cockpit. Then he saw them - two punctures in the starboard hull, just in front of the rear bulkhead. Griff sprang into action, knowing he had less than a minute before the breach blew out the breathable air faster than the life support systems could replenish it. And if the breaches ruptured wider, there was a risk of the cockpit walls collapsing and both of them being blown out into the thin Martian atmosphere.

Griff grabbed the emergency seals and leaped towards the first breach, pressing the magnetized pad to the hull. The hiss of air vanished, but then the ship was rocked by another powerful shimmy, and he was thrown to his back.

"Griff, hurry!" he heard Cutler yell, his voice now lacking any of its normal composure.

Griff pushed himself to his knees and grabbed the back of his head. His fingers were wet with blood and his vision was blurred.

"Griff, seal that breach!" he heard Cutler yell again. He blinked rapidly, trying to clear his vision, and saw the second breach sealing pad on the deck. He crawled towards it and looked up, trying to remember where the puncture in the hull was. The air felt thin and he was struggling to concentrate. He forced himself to stand, though the effort was agonizing, and staggered to the starboard wall. The pressure differential was increasing, pulling his straggly hair towards the opening. Drawing the backing off the pad, he thrust it at the breach, practically crashing against the wall in the process.

The next thing Griff knew, his face was pressed up against a console. Switches and buttons bit into his skin, like the pinch of a dozen tiny crab claws. The hiss of air escaping had stopped, but there was still a fierce roar inside the cabin.

"Griff!" he heard Cutler cry out. He pushed himself off the console, and saw the Martian landscape approaching rapidly through the cockpit glass. "Restart the drives!" Cutler yelled.

Griff lurched towards the second seat and fell into it, before hurriedly fastening his harness. A second later the ventral thrusters overheated, and the nose of the FS-31 dipped towards the red planet's dusty surface. Griff screamed, jamming his feet against the console and digging his fingers into the armrest of the seat. However, his attempts to steel himself against the pressures that were acting on his body were futile, and the FS-31 was still dropping like a stone towards the Martian surface.

"Start the main drives!" Cutler shouted over to Griff. "Five seconds or we're dead!"

The thrusters fired again, and Cutler desperately tried to wrestle the ship into a more controlled descent, but it was as pointless as trying to move a bowling ball by blowing through a straw.

Griff reached for the drive control panel, but it felt like there was a weight attached to his arm, dragging it back. He cried out, using his last ounce of strength, and practically punched his finger through the panel. The roar in the cabin was now met by the rising whine of the main drives spinning back up. Griff's effort had been just enough, and just in time.

"Drives online!" Griff called out, relaxing every muscle in his body, and submitting to the forces that had been fighting to overwhelm him.

They were now only seconds away from smashing into the red Martian surface. Again, powerless to affect his own fate, Griff watched as Cutler slammed the throttle forward, and hauled back on the controls. The forces on Griff's body intensified further, so much so that he was unable even to cry out in pain. He closed his eyes, and almost blacked out, but then suddenly the pressure evaporated. He forced his eyes open and saw that they were hurtling towards a massive, flat-topped mountain.

"Did we make it?" wheezed Griff, still unsure whether the ordeal was over. "Are we safe?" His words came out weak and shaky.

There was an agonizing pause before Cutler finally answered, "Yes. For now."

"Where are we going?" Griff added, scowling at the imposing feature of the Martian landscape as they approached it at speed.

"Arsia Mons," replied Cutler, who now appeared to be fully in control again, though his voice was also breathless and unsteady.

Griff didn't have the strength to question what Arsia Mons was, or why Cutler was heading there. He simply flopped back in his seat and watched the mountain approach. The alarms in the cockpit had mercifully fallen silent, and he could see on his monitors that the MP patrol ships were also nowhere to be seen.

Cutler's crazy stunt had worked. He didn't care how it had worked, only that it had. Griff realized that he should have perhaps trusted Cutler more readily, at least in terms of handling situations such as they had just experienced. Cutler Wendell had made a living out of surviving the seemingly unsurvivable. Though whether this was from luck or judgement, Griff was no longer certain.

Cutler began to climb up the slope of the mountain, before suddenly braking rapidly, and ducking inside a wide pit. The cockpit was thrown into a soothing darkness. Then there was a thud through the deck as the FS-31's landing struts made contact with the Martian surface. Griff heard the engines wind down again, and saw on his panel that Cutler had disabled every non-critical system.

As hiding spots went, even Griff could tell that this was a good one. The shadowy pit would make them impossible to spot from the air, and with most off the systems offline, their power signature was too weak to detect. Unless a patrol craft literally flew directly over their position, they would not be found.

"You've hidden here before?" asked Griff, if only to break the sudden, eerie silence that had fallen over the cockpit.

"Yes," answered Cutler, dimly. Though even with only the light from the cockpit panels illuminating him, Griff could see Cutler's expression was weary and drawn.

Neither spoke for what seemed like several minutes. Griff's muscles burned, and the hair on the back of his head was matted with blood. He was exhausted, dizzy, sore and nauseous – but at least he was alive.

"We must get rid of this ship," said Cutler, eventually breaking the stillness. "The MP will not stop coming for us, because of what happened to the alien moon."

"Then what?" said Griff. "If the MP has a warrant out for us then it's a fair bet the CET does too."

"Will your Superintendent Wash help us?" asked Cutler, but Griff simply shook his head. "The RGF will be blamed for what happened at the new portal world. Wash will deny being involved. Hell, the spiteful witch will probably just try to blame it all on me instead. I still have my RGF credentials, though, for now, at least. My inspector's shield can unlock doors that would otherwise be closed."

The mention of Griff's inspector's shield seemed to get Cutler's attention, and he remained deep in thought for several more seconds.

"I know somewhere that we may be able to lay low," said Cutler, again being the one to break the impasse. "But it will require selling everything we have. And we will need to rely on your RGF credentials to pass through border security, while bypassing the usual CET channels."

Griff shot Cutler a curious glance, "Where do you have in mind?"

"We hide in plain sight," said Cutler. "San Francisco."

Griff laughed and shook his head, but he was too tired to argue. And it wasn't like he had a choice, anymore. Like it or not, Cutler Wendell was now his only hope of escaping a cold, dark holding cell.

"So, where can we get rid of this ship and buy another? One that's off the radar?" asked Griff, accepting his fate.

Cutler glanced back, raising his eyebrows, and Griff could tell he wasn't going to like the answer.

"There is only one place on Mars where we can trade illicitly. Though the terms will not be favorable."

Griff sighed wearily, and then asked, "Where?"

"The shipyards in the Gale Basin," answered Cutler, tentatively.

Griff cursed and sat up, "Are you out of your damn mind?" he shouted. "The Gale Basin? The only place on Mars that's pretty much run by the Council? Who, in case you've forgotten, are the ones trying to kill us!"

"Do you think I want to go there?" replied Cutler, his tongue taking on a sharper edge. "Like it or not, Inspector, the Gale Basin is the only place on Mars where we can trade a ship on the black market."

Griff slumped back into his seat again, and peered up through the darkness into the Martian sky. He reached for a cigarette from the packet in his shirt pocket, but then realized his hands were shaking. Eventually, he managed to wrestle one from the packet and maneuver it to his mouth. It took him three attempts to light it.

How the hell has it come to this? Griff asked himself, drawing deeply on the cigarette. The rush from the nicotine hit gave Griff a sudden lucidity, and the answer presented itself, as clear as the alien crystal that had caused him so much trouble. *Hudson Powell...* he thought, blowing out a plume of smoke above his head, clouding his view of the Martian sky. There was only one person who could have turned him in to the authorities. *It always comes back to Hudson Powell...* he realized. He sucked on the cigarette again and then dug his fingers into the armrest of the chair. Except that this time it was out of rage, not fear. *I'll kill that bastard before this is over,* Griff vowed in that moment, deep inside the Martian pit. *Hudson*

Powell, Liberty Devan and any other piece of shit that follows him. I'll kill them all...

CHAPTER 18

After the discovery of the Earth-like portal worlds, commercial and scientific interest in colonizing Mars disappeared almost overnight. Compared to the warm, breathable atmospheres of the portal worlds, and their Earth-normal gravity, Mars was simply too much effort. Its thin, carbon dioxide atmosphere and cold surface temperatures made it unappealing. However, there were still some on Earth that saw the possibilities of the red planet, not for its resources, but for its potential to start anew.

The rapid technological advancements and rich resources of the new portal worlds quickly made the pioneer explorers rich. From nothing, new mega-corporations quickly grew, based around the reverse-engineered technology from the alien hulks. Several of these powerful corporations then banded together, and applied their combined wealth and commercial expertise to the task of taming Mars. Despite the immense challenges, the advancements in technology, combined with near limitless spending power, allowed a consortium of these powerful business empires to establish the Martian Protectorate.

The new MP declared independence from Earth, sparking a long conflict, which eventually ended in a bitter stalemate. However, the deadlock essentially ensured the MP's sovereignty, and also its claim over all portal worlds, accessed from inside the newly-designated Martian space. The wealth generated from these portal worlds made the consortia even more powerful. As such, Martian society became one where wealth was commonplace and necessary. Only the richest could afford to live there, and only the richest were permitted to. Its inhabitants considered themselves superior to their poor cousins on Earth, and looked down their noses at those from the portal worlds.

Consequently, with the exception of parts of Deimos Station, and the more remote MP portal worlds, Martian space was hostile to hunters, and it was certainly no place for mercenaries, like Cutler Wendell. Yet, for every rule there was always an exception. With a society so uptight and heavily regulated, there always had to be a release valve. A way for those on Mars with a taste for more Earthly decadences to indulge their baser desires. The Gale Basin was that place.

The MP authorities knew about the dealings that went on in the Basin, but they turned a blind eye. In part, this was because many of the Mars super-elite were its biggest customers. However, they also knew that the Basin was necessary, in order to keep any scandal away from polite society. Since none of these leading Martian figures could be associated with the establishments and dealings of the Basin, it was allowed to be run by the Council.

However, compared to the many and varied atrocities and debasements that occurred on places like New Providence, the Basin was a kindergarten. The MP authorities imposed strict restrictions on what the Council could get away with. This was partly down to their primmer sensibilities, but also because they were eager to control the pressure valve manually. A slow release of pressure was enough to maintain a healthy balance, but open the tap too wide, and things would quickly escalate out of control.

Despite this, the Gale Basin was still home to many forms of illegality, and it was still a dangerous place, especially for the unwary. Not everyone who entered the Basin came out unscarred by the experience. Not everyone who entered the Basin came out at all.

Despite the risks, and despite the fact that the Council was hunting for them, Griff had no choice but to accept it was their only option. There was a chance that the Council could be bartered with; Griff knew he would get no such clemency from the CET and MP authorities.

Griff stepped off the rear cargo ramp of the FS-31, and stood beside Cutler. He'd intentionally waited for the mercenary to step off the ship first, making some excuse or other for why he had to delay. The real reason was that he wanted to take the alien crystal out of the now defunct device he'd stolen from Hudson's ship. It had been fractured in half from Tory's wayward bullet, but Griff still wanted to keep it close. Bringing the crystal back to Superintendent Wash might save his ass, he thought. And if not then it could still be used as a bargaining chip with the CET or MP. He might even be able to sell it, relying on his talent for lying to convince any unwitting potential buyer that it wasn't broken at all. Tory's wayward bullet had not created a clean break, and the two halves no longer neatly pieced together. However, no-one else knew what it was supposed to look like, which gave Griff the advantage.

The spaceport was busy with the usual hustle and bustle of commercial traffic, in addition to a host of private shuttles. These had ferried visitors in from the reputable Martian cities, in order to partake in the Basin's unique indulgences.

"What a shit hole," grumbled Griff shaking his head at the place. Griff hated Mars, and he had no love for Martians either. Even the feel of the place was unnatural. Martians preferred the temperature always a little too hot for Griff's liking, and he could somehow even taste the manufactured fakeness of the place in the air. Even the gravity felt wrong. Adapted from technology discovered on the alien hulks, the artificial gravity wells that enveloped Martian cities felt clingy and invasive. It was like being anchored to the floor by elasticated rubber straps. "Can we get this done and leave as quickly as possible?" he grumbled, already regretting stepping off the ship. "This place makes my skin crawl."

Cutler pressed a button on his ID fob to close the FS-31's rear ramp, then thumbed the credit scanner to pay the docking fee. Griff noticed that the registry ID of Cutler's ship did not flash up on the credit scanner's screen. The mercenary had stealthed their ID before taking off from Arsia Mons. Ordinarily, this would prohibit them from entering any Martian space port, but since anonymity was a key feature of the Gale Basin, they had been permitted to dock. Nevertheless, Griff knew that the MP could still trace their movements. Cutler may have been able to stealth their ID, but an FS-31 Patrol Craft was a ship that tended to stick out in a crowd.

"The person we need to find is an ex-hunter called Miranda Yaeger," said Cutler, glancing anxiously around the docking garage. "Like you, she shares the curious penchant for being referred to by her last name."

Cutler's edginess was making Griff immediately uncomfortable. He also began to peer around the docking garage, suddenly seeing phantom Council assassins and MP officers lurking in every dark nook and cranny. Then he saw an MP patrol ship docked in the far corner, and his heart leapt. He quickly turned his back to it and steered Cutler so that he also faced away. The mercenary shook him off, and glowered at him.

"Take it easy, Cutler," said Griff, staring back with matching venom. "There's an MP patrol back there; I'm just trying to make sure we're not seen."

Cutler glanced behind briefly, before his eyes resumed their usual poker-faced inexpressiveness. "They are likely here for the same reasons as the others. But all the same, we should proceed with caution."

"Apology accepted," muttered Griff, plucking a cigarette from the packet in his pocket. He noticed he was down to his last two. He lit it and motioned for Cutler to lead the way. "So, let's go and find this Yaeger person so we can get off this dusty rock."

Cutler led them out of the docking garage and onto the long boulevard that eventually joined up to the central precinct. It was one of four such boulevards in the Basin; one for each of the four quadrants of the domed, circular city.

The boulevard was one of the ritzier parts of the Gale Basin. It was lined with bars, massage parlors, gambling dens and worse, all designed to capture the eager traveler. In many ways, it wasn't unlike a scavenger town, Griff realized. And like the scavenger towns, Griff knew that the best and the worst that the Basin had to offer were likely to be found in the more off-beat places.

Cutler hailed an autonomous ground cab, and got in. Griff scowled, and sucked in the remains of his cigarette, before tossing the stub to the floor. He blew out the smoke and then climbed in beside Cutler. "I hate these damn things," he complained, fidgeting to get comfortable in the seat. "I prefer to be the one in charge."

Cutler glanced over at Griff. He seemed to be growing more and more irritated by Griff's comments and complaints. "But you're not in charge, anymore, Inspector," Cutler said, darkly. "If I were you, I wouldn't forget that."

"And what the hell is that supposed to mean?" Griff hit back, but Cutler didn't answer, and instead just pulled the cab's microphone closer.

"Quadrant four, section thirteen," said Cutler, before resting back in the seat.

Griff watched him out of the corner of his eye for a time, mulling over what Cutler had said. Though it was often difficult to determine Cutler's true meaning, due to the monotone way he spoke, to Griff it had sounded like a warning, or even a threat. Cutler still needed Griff's money, and his influence to get back to Earth. However, he also knew that there would soon come a time when Griff was merely an encumbrance. Cutler's veiled warning – whether intended or otherwise – served to remind Griff that they weren't friends, or allies. Cutler wouldn't hesitate to kill Griff when the time was right, and he needed to be ready to strike first.

The cab trundled on through the Basin's narrow streets, then turned a corner to join one of the main transitways. "How well do you know this Yaeger woman?" said Griff. It was partly to fill the silence, but he was also curious to find out what information the secretive mercenary was willing to divulge. "Can you trust her?"

"I don't trust anyone," said Cutler, flatly. "I only trust what motivates people."

"Oh, and so what motivates her?" said Griff, intrigued by Cutler's cryptic reply.

"Getting the better of me," replied Cutler, flatly. "I once cost her a lot. She will enjoy getting her payback."

Suddenly the cab was rocked from the side and Griff's head was slammed against the window. He grabbed the door handle to steady himself and touched a hand to his head, again feeling blood. He cursed and peered out through the cracked glass. Another ground transit had just rammed them. Two men were inside, and Griff could see the barrels of weapons poking up above the window line.

"Shit!" Griff shouted, looking into Cutler's wide eyes. "It's the Council – they've found us!"

CHAPTER 19

The Council vehicle suddenly veered towards the autonomous ground cab for a second time, and Griff steeled himself against the impending impact. "Hold on!" he shouted to Cutler, as the lightweight cab was rocked again.

This time the impact was hard enough to drive them into the safety barrier. The cab rebounded off the metal wall, then spun out of control. Griff held on tightly, the street outside merely a blur, before the cab collided with the safety barrier at an intersection and came to a jarring halt. Griff flew forward and bounced off the rear of the front seat, before tumbling down into the footwell. Blinking the pain from his head, he looked up to see Cutler slumped back in his seat, blood trickling from his temple. The mercenary appeared to still be conscious, but was heavily stunned.

Griff clawed his way off the floor of the cab and peered out of the smashed front window. The other ground transit had pulled up about twenty meters ahead and the two men were getting out. Both wore smart suits with a typical Martian cut. However, both also carried compact SMGs, of the sort than only one organization regularly used – the Council.

"Cutler, get up!" Griff yelled, staying low. Cutler didn't answer, so Griff reached over and grabbed the mercenary's jacket, shaking him vigorously. "Cutler, wake up, it's the Council!" he shouted again, but Cutler's head just lolled back and forth. "Shit!" Griff swore, before reaching over and pulling the door release on Cutler's side. The door swung open and Cutler fell out onto the tarmacked road like a rag doll.

Griff then heard the rattle of the SMGs as the Council goons opened fire, and he flattened himself to the footwell again. Fractured glass from the rear and side windows peppered his head and body as the bullets thudded into the cab. He reached into his jacket and pulled out the sidearm he'd concealed there, before crawling out of the open door. Another volley of gunfire rattled against the cab's metal chassis and punctured through the seats. If Griff had waited only a few seconds longer before moving, he'd already be dead.

Griff quickly checked on Cutler, but he was still groggy, and unable to stand. Staying low, and using the cab as cover, he dragged Cutler behind the junction barrier they had crashed into.

Griff's heart was pumping so hard it hurt his chest. He remained crouched behind the barrier, waiting for the men to launch another assault. Seconds later, he heard the weapons open fire, and the rattle of metal as dozens more bullets turned the cab into something more closely resembling a kitchen sieve. He'd got lucky; the Council thugs evidently hadn't seen him slip out.

Taking a deep breath, he stood up and aimed. The goons were working their way around the side of the cab, carefully checking inside. Griff held his breath and fired. The first few shots missed, but then the nearest of the two Council thugs was hit twice in the neck and shoulder. He was thrown back against the cab, before he slid to the road, leaving a smear of blood on the bullet-riddled door.

Griff continued firing until he was empty, then released his empty magazine before reaching for another. The second Council thug then jumped up from behind the cab, and raised his weapon. Griff ducked behind the barrier instinctively, as bullets pinged into the metal partition. The magazine fell from his hand and skated off down the slip road.

"Shit!" Griff roared into the stuffy Martian air. Then he remembered that Cutler also still carried his weapon and crawled back to the mercenary's side. However, before he could reach him, the Council thug appeared on the other side of the barrier, and aimed the barrel of the SMG at his chest. Griff froze and raised his hands, before the crack of gunfire rang out again. The goon fell forwards, blood draining from beneath his chin. Griff looked down to see Cutler, back pressed against the safety barrier. His weapon was aimed upwards, and smoke oozed from the barrel.

"We have to move, now," said Cutler, still woozy. "More will come."

Griff didn't need telling twice. He darted down the slip road to collect his wayward magazine, and reloaded his weapon, before recovering the empty magazine and sliding it back into his pocket. He then raced back to Cutler and helped him to his feet.

"We can take their transit," said Cutler, spotting the Council vehicle by the side of the road. There were sirens in the distance, but other transits were still blocking the road behind them.

Griff set off towards the transit, stepping over the dead body of the Council thug. His tailored suit jacket had flopped open, and tucked inside the inner pocket was a black packet of cigarettes. Griff paused and yanked them out of the dead man's pocket. "I'll take those, you piece of shit," he snarled, kicking the dead body in the side.

"Hurry!" Cutler called back to him, as the mercenary edged around the vehicle. He was still moving sluggishly, and blood continued to trickle down the side of his face.

Griff ran to the vehicle and dropped into the driver's seat, before slamming the door shut. A few seconds later, Cutler slumped into the seat at his side.

"Which way?!" cried Griff, starting the vehicle's engine.

"Double back, and take the lower slip road," said Cutler, dabbing blood from his head with his sleeve. "We'll take the subterranean roads. It's slower, but it should avoid the MP police, and any more trouble from the Council."

Griff nodded, then spun the transit around, before driving the wrong way down the road, and turning off along the slip road. He noticed Cutler reach forward and press the door lock button on the center console.

"Don't worry, I'm not planning to get out of this thing until we reach the shipyard," said Griff, wondering why Cutler had locked the doors. "And I just saved your ass, so I'm not likely to kick you out now!"

Cutler rested back again, and peered out of the window. "It's not to stop us getting out," he said, flatly. "It's to stop anyone else from getting in."

Griff scowled at him, "I'll probably regret asking you this, but who would want to get in?"

Cutler continued to dab blood from his head, before glancing back at Griff. "Not everyone who enters the Basin leaves as rich as they were when they entered," he said, ominously. "And for those who lose everything, they end up down here. Trust me when I say, you don't want to get out, and you don't want to let anyone else in."

Griff laughed, nervously. "I really hope whatever this Yaeger has against you is enough to get us a new ship," he said, following the nav chart and taking a right turn. "Because I've had it with this shitty place already."

Three shadowy figures lurked on the corner as Griff slowed, each of them watching the vehicle closely as it passed by. Griff quickly sped up again, taking the corner faster than he would have liked. After Cutler's warning, his sense of urgency had been ratcheted up a notch.

"She will provide what we need," replied Cutler. Then he looked at Griff, his eyes suddenly sharper and more serious, "But it will cost us."

"How much?" asked Griff, steering to avoid another cluster of suspect-looking pedestrians, huddled by the roadside.

Cutler waited for Griff to meet his eyes, before he answered. Then with a chilling finality, he said, "It will cost both of us everything we have to give."

CHAPTER 20

On Cutler's advice, Griff had stopped their stolen vehicle before exiting the subterranean layer of the Basin. To drive it back up to the surface layer would risk them being spotted by surveillance cameras or drones. It was far less likely they'd be identified on foot, especially once they had made it inside section thirteen. The shipyard district was always bustling, and it was also one of the Council's most lucrative businesses. As such, the MP police in the city treated the goings-on in the district with a relatively light touch. This allowed the various black-market deals to proceed, unhindered by their intimidating presence.

"How far is it to the shipyard from here?" asked Griff, sliding open the door and stepping outside. He held his pistol ready, and carefully checked the dark corners of the underpass for any signs of movement.

Cutler got out and went to the rear of the transit. "Not far," he answered, throwing open the trunk and searching inside. "This section of road is disused, to regular traffic, at least. But we can pass through one of the service maintenance areas into section thirteen from here."

Griff scowled at Cutler, who was still rifling through the contents of the trunk. "What the hell are you doing in there?" he called over. "We need to get moving."

Cutler removed something from the trunk and moved around to Griff's side, before holding out an ID card to him. "This is a counterfeit ID," he said, as Griff took the card. "Knowing the Council, it will likely open most doors, including the service hatches."

Cutler then adjusted his hold on the object he'd taken from the vehicle, and Griff finally got a better look at it. Curiously, it appeared to be a standard black leather briefcase. Watching with interest, Griff observed as Cutler placed the briefcase on the floor and opened it. He squinted in the gloom to get a better look inside. There was a sidearm, which Cutler took and slid down the back of his pants, and an assortment of metal tools. Griff suddenly realized what it was. "Is that a damn torture kit?" he said, shuddering a little at the thought that it had been intended to be used on them.

"Yes," answered Cutler, pulling out a white bottle of pills and a small spray can. "But they always include some simple medical supplies too." Cutler stood up, popped open the bottle and swallowed some of the pills. He then pocketed the bottle and sprayed the aerosol on the cut to the side of his head. The bleeding immediately stopped.

"During the process of interrogation, it is always helpful to keep your victim alive and cognizant for as long as possible," mused Cutler. He then placed the spray bottle into his pocket too. "To do so increases the chances of extracting valuable information, before unconsciousness or death."

Griff laughed at the laid-back, yet macabre manner in which Cutler had described the purpose of the briefcase. However, he was also slightly uncomfortable at how much Cutler seemed to know about it. "These Council assholes are dark, but they're smart, I'll give them that," said Griff. He wanted to play it tough, so that Cutler didn't think him squeamish. "Maybe I'm starting to like them."

Cutler didn't appear to be amused or impressed by Griff's bravado, "You would not say that if you saw what the Council interrogators did with these implements, Inspector."

Griff shrugged, "Yeah, well keep hold of that briefcase; it will come in handy when I finally catch up with Powell."

"You would not have the stomach for it," answered Cutler, derisively. He then closed the briefcase, and left it on the damp concrete floor. "You think you are as hard and as remorseless as these people, but you are nothing like them, Inspector Griff. You have no idea who you're dealing with, and you're way out of your depth."

"What did you just say?" said Griff, lowering his weapon to his side, and turning to face Cutler. He was surprised and angered by the mercenary's sudden show of contempt for him. Especially after Griff had just saved his skin.

"I apologize if the truth hurts, Inspector," said Cutler, though it did not sound like an apology. "But I'm tired of your bullshit. You're just a sadist that likes to pick the wings off flies. You think that makes you a killer, but you're just a bully." Then Cutler pointed to Griff's ID wallet, attached to his belt. "You hide behind the protection offered by that shield, but it will not help you here. And if your Superintendent Jane Wash decides to make an example of you, it will not protect you anywhere else either."

Griff leaned in towards Cutler and glared into his cold, impassive eyes. "I don't need any damn protection," he spat back. "I'm a survivor," he added, pointing his yellowed finger and tapping his chest angrily. "And if you keep pissing me off, you'll see just how much of a killer I really am."

Cutler stared into Griff's eyes, without blinking. "We shall see, Inspector," said the mercenary, making it sound almost like a challenge. "But understand this; without me, you wouldn't survive here on your own for more than a couple of hours. Do not forget that." Cutler then turned away and walked into the center of the slip-road, leaving Griff stunned and lost for words.

Griff peered up the ramp at the light from the pinkish sky, filtered through the protective dome, and set off after the mercenary. Then he caught a glimpse of a shadow moving in the darkness across the other side of the road. He raised his weapon, and a boy shuffled out of the gloom; he was perhaps no more than twelve or thirteen.

"Get out of here, kid," Griff called over to him, but the boy just cupped his hands and held them out. Griff lowered his weapon, but then raised the back of his hand. "I mean it, get lost, I've got nothing for you."

There was a sharp crack of a weapon firing, and Griff jolted around to see Cutler aiming into the darkness. The boy ran, and Griff saw the body of a man fall out of the shadows, from behind one of the support pillars. A pistol slid from his fingers, and skidded across the tarmac.

Griff watched Cutler lower his pistol and look at him. He realized he still had his hand raised, ready to strike the boy, despite the fact the rogue had already fled into the darkness.

"You did save my life, earlier," said Cutler, holstering his weapon, "but now we are even." Then Cutler turned and started to ascend the disused slip-road, back up to the surface level of the Gale Basin.

Griff stared at the body for a moment longer, then shoved the pistol back into his jacket pocket. "We'll see who is the greater survivor," he muttered under his breath, watching Cutler climb higher. Griff glanced at the briefcase, fleetingly contemplating picking it up, if only to prove a point, but then turned from it, and followed after Cutler.

Half-way up the slip-road, he cast an eye back to the body of the anonymous man that Cutler had shot. His death didn't bother him, nor had the deaths of the two Council thugs, or anyone else he'd killed in the past. Griff had never been afraid to kill, if it got him what he wanted. However, Cutler had been right about one thing, and he cursed him for it. Because now Cutler had planted a kernel of doubt in his mind.

The RGF had provided Griff with a safety net, and it was true that he'd always done what he'd done knowing that the uniform protected him. And, if the shit really did hit the fan, he also knew that Wash would be there to back him up, even if it cost him in credits and favors. Because of this, he'd never really felt fear. Cutler had made him realize that all of this armor was rapidly eroding away. And without it, Griff was also ashamed to realize that for the first time in his life, he was truly afraid.

CHAPTER 21

Cutler had been right about the counterfeit ID he'd taken from the Council transport. Using it, Griff had managed to open a door to a service corridor that led directly into section thirteen. It had given them access to the shipyard district without needing to pass through the usual junction points. This had allowed them to avoid the facial ID scanners that might have alerted the Council to their new location. Importantly, the facial ID scanners were not active inside the shipyard district, in order to protect the identities of those dealing illicitly inside. Griff hoped that this would give them the window of opportunity they needed to acquire a new ship and escape.

Cutler had said little since the incident in the subterranean slip road, but Griff was in no mood to talk anyway. Their alliance remained intact, though it was more fragile than ever. The only thing that mattered was getting a new ship – one that was totally untraceable – and getting away from Mars. Then he would lay low on Earth and wait for the storm to blow over. He was sure that the CET and MP armadas would eventually deal with the titanic alien ship. And once the dust had settled, he'd reach out to Wash. If she refused to help him out of this mess, he'd try to do a deal with the CET instead. With the dirt he had on Wash – both her personal and professional deviances – plus the fact he could also turn over Cutler Wendell, he was sure there was a deal to be done. However, all of it relied on him escaping from the Basin, before the Council caught up with them again. After the destruction of Chrome One, and with the knowledge that he'd have to hand over his score to get a new ship, doing a deal with the Council now seemed a near impossibility.

"Yaeger's shipyard is in that lot," said Cutler, pointing to one of the many sectioned-off areas in the shipyard district. The whole place was like one giant parking lot, subdivided by low walls or makeshift barricades, which marked out the boundaries of the different ship dealers. There were repair hangars and workshops lining the fringes, plus the usual eateries and bars. It felt like a giant festival for spacecraft enthusiasts.

They entered Yaeger's lot, and Griff scanned his eyes over some of the stock on display. Compared to the ships he could see on other nearby lots,

Yaeger's offerings seemed to be scraping the bottom of the bargain bucket.

"Can't we buy a ship from one of these other places?" wondered Griff, gesturing to the many other, better options around them. "I'd be surprised if any of Yaeger's hunks of crap could even make orbit."

Cutler shot Griff an impatient look. "None of these other dealers will touch my ship now," he said, making no attempt to hide his irritation. "Not after your mission made us the galaxy's most wanted men. My FS-31 is simply too hot."

"I didn't do a damn thing," Griff hit back. "It was your nutjob partner that messed up the crystal device. If we still had that, we'd still have some negotiating power. So, don't blame me for this mess!"

Cutler shook his head, "I wish I had never answered your call on Brahms Three," he answered, bitterly. "You have caused me nothing but trouble. Once we reach San Francisco, I will be glad to finally part ways."

"Yeah, well you and me both," Griff hit back. Then he pointed to a nearby shuttle that had fluid dripping steadily out from its fuselage. "But do you really want to go to Earth in that?"

Cutler didn't look at the shuttle; he was focused on a trailer office about thirty meters away. "We have no choice. Yaeger's stock may not be the best, but here we are not compelled to register our actual names and biometric scans. Nor do we have to add the ship's ID to the public registry." He then glanced at Griff and added, condescendingly, "But, if you want the Council to identify us and shoot us down the moment we depart, be my guest and select another lot."

Griff plucked out a cigarette from the packet he had removed from the dead Council thug's body and stuck it into the corner of his mouth, "Fine, we'll do it your way," he conceded, before lighting the smoke. "Just so long as Yaeger doesn't hate you enough to sell you a crapped out, cut-and-shut job."

A woman stepped out of the trailer office unit inside the lot, and then stood looking at them, hands on her hips. Cutler did not acknowledge her in any way, and turned to Griff. "Let me do the talking," he said, forcefully, as the woman began to walk towards them.

Griff drew deeply on the cigarette and blew out a plume of smoke. He didn't like that Cutler was giving him orders now, but he bit his tongue. So long as the mercenary secured a ship that didn't blow up before reaching Earth, he didn't care. Cutler would get his due eventually.

"You can turn around right now, you double-crossing asshole," said Yaeger, stopping a few meters from Cutler and folding her arms. Griff continued to smoke, enjoying the embarrassed look on Cutler's face. He'd immediately taken a liking to the woman. She and Cutler were probably a similar age, but Yaeger was much rougher around the edges. She'd probably clean up pretty well, Griff thought, checking her out casually. However, she was what the Martians ironically called an 'alien'. It was a term given to someone who was too crude and uncouth to fit in to Martian society, no matter how rich they were. If it wasn't for the Basin, Yaeger wouldn't have been allowed anywhere near the red planet.

Yaeger glanced over to Griff, who realized he was smiling. "And what are you looking at, beanpole?" she snapped. "Peep shows are over on the boulevards."

Griff opened his mouth to speak, but Cutler got there first. "Yaeger, just give me a minute, I promise it will be worth your while."

"Oh, really?" said Yaeger, recoiling slightly. "Like when you said it would be 'worth my while' to hunt with you on Debussy Seven?" Then before Cutler could respond, Yaeger looked at Griff again, and said, "I don't suppose he told you how he swindled me out of my score and left me for dead?" She paused as if waiting for Griff to answer, but then continued anyway. "Or how he stole my bloody ship?" Again, she looked at Griff expectantly for an answer, but didn't give him an opportunity to provide one.

Yaeger then turned back to Cutler. "What happened to your other lacky? The one who could freeze a man's balls off with her icy stare? Assuming she hadn't cut them off first."

"The ship is why I'm here," Cutler replied, ignoring Yaeger's other questions, particularly the one about Tory. "I want to trade it to you."

Yaeger left another pregnant pause, then burst out laughing in Cutler's face. "You must be shitting me? Why would I buy my own ship – that you stole – back off you?"

Cutler removed a small datapad from his pocket, and held it out to Yaeger. "Because I need your help," he said, calmly, still waiting for Yaeger to take the pad.

The woman laughed again, then finally snatched the device from Cutler's hand. Clearly, curiosity had gotten the better of her. "You've come to the wrong place if you want help," Yaeger said, turning on the datapad and staring at the contents. Griff could just about make out that it was the FS-31's manifest.

"I need a ship that is capable of travelling to Earth at reasonable speed," Cutler continued, while Yaeger read the manifest. "Any ship, even of considerably lesser value than the FS-31, providing it can safely reach Earth." Yaeger was silent for a moment, and was scowling down at the pad. "In return, I offer the FS-31 and its entire cargo."

Yaeger let the pad drop to her side and scowled back at Cutler. "You're including all of this alien shit, and the ship?" she asked, sounding skeptical.

Cutler merely nodded. "And I can give you any one-g capable ship or shuttle from my lot in return?" Cutler nodded again.

Yaeger laughed. "You're in some sort of trouble, ain't you? You came here because you needed something off grid. And you thought I'd help, because I'd enjoy ripping you off and rubbing your face in it?"

Cutler sighed, and then said, "Was I wrong?"

Yaeger snorted and slapped the datapad against her oil-stained cargo pants. "Nope! You're dead right, asshole!" Then she laughed again. "What is it, some Council trouble?" Cutler didn't answer, but then Yaeger seemed to have an epiphany. "Wait a minute, haven't I heard about you two?" she said, rubbing her chin and smearing oil across it. "You and the asshole with the slug on his top lip are the ones who found that new portal. The one that's sent the MP and CET militaries into a tizzy, right?"

"Do you want the deal or not?" growled Cutler, and Griff could clearly see now that he was losing patience. As much as Griff had been enjoying seeing Cutler brought down a peg or two, he was also anxious to get going. Besides, Yaeger was now leveling insults indiscriminately at him too, and his tolerance for abuse was considerably lower than Cutler's was.

"Oh, I want the deal, asshole," she said, suddenly becoming more serious. "But it's going to cost you something extra. I want that alien crystal I've heard about too. Rumor has it, that's the thing that opens portals."

Griff felt a lump harden in his throat, but he didn't react. Glancing over to Cutler, he saw that his expression also gave nothing away.

"I no longer have it," Cutler replied, coolly. "The RGF took it back from me, after we opened the portal to Chrome One."

Yaeger's eyes narrowed and her jaw sharpened. "Now, now, Cutler. I thought we were starting afresh here? Lying to me will likely mean our business dealings won't end well."

Cutler did not flinch. "The deal is the FS-31, plus all of the alien artefacts in the hold – the value of which is considerable. You walk away from this significantly richer, and you get to humble me. What more could you want?"

"I want that damn crystal," said Yaeger, and the corner of her mouth turned up a fraction as she added, "and another one hundred thousand for my trouble."

Cutler's eyes narrowed, but he held firm. "Now you are being ridiculous. I told you, I do not have it..."

Yaeger shrugged and blew out an elaborate sigh. "Then no deal. Good luck trading your ship off-grid with one of the other dealers," she said, turning around and walking back to her trailer office. "Especially after I tell them how hot your FS-31 is with the Martian authorities..."

Griff could see Cutler's hands ball into fists, and for a second he thought he was going for his weapon. *Shit...* he thought. He'd underestimated just how prideful Cutler was.

"Wait!" Griff called out to Yaeger, causing both her and Cutler to stare at him. He tossed his half-smoked cigarette to the floor and then reached into his jacket pocket. Removing one half of the fractured crystal, he held it out to Yaeger, "Here, take the damned thing," he said, reluctantly. "And I'll give you the credits too."

Yaeger smiled and sashayed back over to them, before wagging a mocking finger at Cutler. "See, I knew you were lying," she said, clearly loving every moment of her revenge. "You haven't changed a bit."

Griff stepped closer, still holding out the crystal fragment. "He wasn't lying," he said, as Yaeger turned to him. "The RGF did reclaim the crystal. I'm RGF." Then he took the ID wallet off his belt, and showed Yaeger his card and shield.

Yaeger looked at the ID and nodded, before smiling up at Griff. "From what I hear, after your little stunt at Chrome One, that pretty little shield won't be worth the metal it's made from soon."

Griff gritted his teeth and fastened the ID back to his belt. He held up the crystal again, "Do we have a deal?"

Griff had more than enough credits from selling Liberty to the Council. He still begrudged handing them over, but the bigger issue was parting with the crystal fragment. Without both halves of the crystal, Griff knew his negotiating position with Wash would be pretty much non-existent. However, the other crystal fragment, plus turning in Cutler, and offering to air Wash's dirty laundry, might still be enough to get him a deal with the CET authorities. It was a chance he was willing to take.

Yaeger held Griff's eyes for a moment, soaking up all of his obvious discomfort like warm rays of sunlight, before her moment of triumph was over. Then she plucked the crystal from Griff's fingers and shoved it into her breast pocket.

Griff pointed a nicotine-stained finger at Yaeger, "But if I'm giving you the credits too, you'd better not offload some hunk of crap shuttle on me, like that one over there." Griff moved his finger in the direction of the leaking ship.

"Relax clobber," said Yaeger, "I'll give you something that will make it back to Earth." Then she smiled again, "But after that, I ain't making any promises."

Griff scowled at her, but Yaeger had already turned her grinning face towards Cutler. She held out her hand, making a sort of grabbing motion with it. Cutler sighed again, and removed the FS-31's ID fob from his belt. Pressing his thumb to the fob, and holding it up to his eye, he reset the ownership data, then slapped it into Yaeger's hand.

Yaeger smiled even more broadly, before waving the ID fob at Cutler, like a trophy. "Now, asshole, we have a deal."

CHAPTER 22

Morphus had accompanied Liberty inside its ship, and begun the augmentation that would allow her to pilot the prototype Revocater. Tobin had gone with her; his first duty in his role as Liberty's moral support. Tory, meanwhile, was still inside the Orion, running the launch checklist along with some diagnostics, and generally getting acquainted with the ship. Hudson, on the other hand, found himself alone and at a loose end.

His first thought was to take a moment to reflect on everything that had happened. However, the enormity of recent events, plus the scale of what they still had to do, was too much to take in. In many ways, the less he thought about the magnitude of the task ahead of them, the better. So, instead, he'd decided to unplug and unwind, for as long as he could get away with it.

Hudson was sitting on the grass in front of the Orion, resting back against a rock with an ice-bucket of beers at his side. The sky had cleared, the wind had eased, and the sun was starting to set. Yet, despite the autumn freshness in the air, he didn't feel cold. The nearby scavenger town was also ominously silent, due to most of the hunters having fled in a panic. As a result, the planet felt oddly peaceful, despite essentially being on the front line of the impending battle with Goliath.

"Are you going to toss me one of those?"

Hudson looked around to see Tory perched on one of the rocks behind him. He hadn't considered stealth to be one of the brash mercenary's core attributes, but she had snuck up on him with ease.

"How do you like the Orion?" Hudson replied, holding up a bottle. Tory took it and slipped down by his side against the rock.

"It's a good ship," Tory answered, taking a swig of the beer.

Hudson waited for Tory to continue with a more detailed assessment, but it soon became apparent that, 'it's a good ship' was the extent of her evaluation. "Well, I'm glad you like it," replied Hudson, smiling. "The big question is, where do we take it next? You said you could find Cutler?"

Tory took another swig of the beer then rested the bottle on her thigh. "We set up a few bolt holes dotted around the core worlds and portal worlds, where we could lay low if needed," Tory began, staring off towards the sunset. "He could have gone to any one of them, but my hunch is that he'll head back to Earth."

Tory's answer surprised Hudson. "Why Earth, surely that would be one of the last places he'd go?" asked Hudson. "Especially with Commodore Trent putting out a warrant for his arrest."

"On the portal worlds, there are only so many places to hide," Tory continued. "Scavenger towns and space stations are easy to search, and even if you hide out in the wilderness, eventually you have to surface for supplies." Tory took another swig of her beer, then glanced at Hudson. "And Mars is no place for someone like him. If he can get to Earth without being detected, it would be like finding a needle in a haystack."

Hudson nodded. What Tory had said made sense, but he still didn't understand how Cutler could make it back when Trent was amassing an armada at Earth. "That's assuming he can get to Earth undetected," said Hudson, "so, I'm guessing he had a plan for that too?"

Tory nodded, "He'll have to ditch his ship first, and get a new one. Something unregistered and off-grid."

"The Gale Basin?" suggested Hudson, and Tory's eyes widened. He was even sure he detected the hint of a smile.

"You know the place?" asked Tory, while spinning the neck of her beer bottle between her fingers.

"Unfortunately, yes," replied Hudson, recalling the numerous times he'd been required to do courier runs to the decadent city. "The locals call it 'The Scar on Mars'. Though, on second thoughts, it's exactly the sort of place Griff would fit in."

"It's run by the Council," said Tory, taking another swig, then tossing the empty bottle onto the grass by her feet.

"Sounds right up his street then," said Hudson. He slipped her another beer without being asked, and she took it. "Lots more shady assholes for him to mingle with."

Tory shook her head, "The Council are looking for Cutler and Griff, because of New Providence," she said, again playing with the neck of the bottle. "And they're looking for me too. They think we double-crossed the Council and helped Liberty to escape, after taking their money."

Hudson raised his beer bottle to Tory, like a salute. "Which you did. That's something neither of us will ever forget, you know..."

Tory sighed, but didn't acknowledge Hudson's gesture, or his admiration for what she'd done. "Being indentured to the Council is something I wouldn't wish on anyone." Then she gave a little shrug, and added, "Well, perhaps apart from scum like Griff."

Hudson grabbed another beer from the ice bucket and popped off the cap. Something Tory said had made him think, and he realized how little he still knew about her. "It sounds like you have some personal experience of how the Council treats people," he said. He was careful not to phrase it as a question, but leave it open for Tory to elaborate if she wanted to.

There was silence between them for a time, while they both watched the sun drop lower over the horizon.

"I was sold to the Council when I was eleven," Tory said, taking Hudson completely by surprise. There was no strain in her voice, and her cheeks had not flushed a brighter color. She had said the words with no more difficulty than if she were reading a ship's diagnostic report. "The Council has many uses for the indentured, but they realized that my particular talent was violence." Then she looked at Hudson, and her eyes were even colder and harder than he was used to seeing. "They discovered this some years later, when I clawed the eyes out of one of their customers."

"Why?" said Hudson, too stunned to know what else to say.

"Because he tried to use me for one of the other purposes that the Council has for those in their service," replied Tory, before taking a casual swig from her bottle.

"I'm sorry," said Hudson, again at a loss for what else to say.

"They were going to kill me, but I disarmed the guard and shot him first," Tory went on. Hudson was surprised at her sudden frankness, and while it was tough to hear her story, he was glad Tory felt she could tell him. "Then I took his knife and killed the other guard. I was about to gut my bastard holder too, until Cutler stopped me."

Hudson almost dropped his beer. "Cutler was there?"

Tory took another swig, and then nodded. "He was a hired bodyguard for the client at that time."

"Not a very good one, as it turned out," said Hudson, still struggling to accept what he was hearing. "Why did he stop you?"

Tory shrugged, "I never asked. But if I'd have killed my holder, the Council would likely have just stormed the room and gunned us both down. Maybe he saw it as the only way to save his own ass."

Hudson laughed under his breath, "He does have a talent for self-preservation, I'll give him that."

"As a reward for saving my holder's life, the Council handed my fate to Cutler." She had already almost finished her second beer. "I said I'd rather die than be owned by anyone again, and I was ready to go down fighting. But instead of killing me, or choosing to own me himself, he offered to buy my relcase," Tory continued.

Hudson was beginning to understand the relationship between Cutler and Tory, and why Tory had been so reticent to abandon the mercenary.

"The client was incensed; he wanted me to suffer for what I'd done," Tory went on, still talking freely and without emotion. "He took the knife that I'd used to kill the guard and came at me."

"Then what happened?" said Hudson. He was almost reticent to hear more, but morbid curiosity got the better of him and he had to know.

"Cutler killed him," replied Tory, briefly meeting Hudson's eyes. "The Council saw it as a just intervention, considering they had given Cutler the power to decide what happened to me. It only served to enhance his reputation in their eyes."

"So, Cutler set you free instead, and you felt indebted to him?" suggested Hudson, taking a guess at the next part of her story.

"Cutler is many things, but a fool he is not," said Tory, though this time Hudson could detect a hint of resentment in her voice. "In his line of work, someone like me would prove to be very useful," she added, a little more sullenly. "I owed him, and doing the jobs he needed seemed better than being dead. At least I was free." Then she tossed the second empty bottle to the ground and held Hudson's eyes. "I told you I was someone you don't want to know. Now you understand why."

Hudson looked back to the horizon, stroking his thumb across his chin idly, as he let Tory's words filter through his mind. Then he turned back to her and smiled. "I never thought you were a saint, Tory," he began, "and I couldn't begin to understand the life you've had. But whatever you were; whatever they made you – that's not who I see. And I never have done." He smiled and raised his bottle, "Now, you really are free. Free to be the person you want to be. The real Tory Bellona."

"Griff always did say you were a dumb rook," replied Tory, her expression as inflexible as iron.

Hudson scowled, "Hey, that's a low blow!" he complained. "I was being nice."

"I'm not used to people being nice."

Hudson took another beer from the cooler, and offered it to her. "Well, you'd better start getting used to it."

Tory laughed, but rather than her usual cruel or derisive laugh, this one seemed natural. It was a shock to hear Tory laugh this way, and it changed her entire visage. It was a good look on her, Hudson thought, smiling.

Tory took the beer, before adding, a little more playfully. "Are you trying to get me drunk, Hudson Powell?"

"Not with this piss-water," laughed Hudson. "But you've drunk all of my whisky already."

Tory smiled, and in that brief moment, it was like she was a different person; someone not weighed down with years of heavy baggage. Tory popped the cap off the beer, took a swig, then handed it back to Hudson.

Hudson took a sip and then, emboldened by Tory's sudden candor, tried his luck with another question. It was one that had been at the back of his mind ever since their encounter in the medical bay.

"We never talked about that kiss," he said, offering the beer back to Tory.

"What's to talk about?" she replied, taking the bottle from Hudson's hand.

Hudson shrugged, realizing he hadn't the faintest idea what he expected Tory to say. Or even what he hoped her answer would be. Then he threw up a hand and said, "I guess I'm wondering if you're going to stick around long enough for there to be another one."

Tory grabbed Hudson's jacket, pulled him closer and kissed him again. Just like the first time she'd done it, he was totally unprepared. And, just like the first time, someone arrived to interrupt them.

"My apologies," said Morphus, standing just behind the rocks. Hudson recoiled, wondering just how long the alien entity had been standing there, watching. "I did not mean to intrude in your pre-coital mating ritual."

Hudson practically fell over backwards. "Pre-coital what?" he stammered, feeling his cheeks burning. "No, we were just... well, we were..."

"Yes, you did interrupt our pre-coital mating ritual," said Tory, completely straight-faced. Hudson's mouth fell open, but Tory was too focused on Morphus to spot it. "So how about you get to the point, lady? Quickly..."

Morphus raised its eyebrows in what was a perfect simulation of an affronted expression. "Very well, I came to discuss your next steps, once I depart for the Revocater with the Liberty Devan and Tobin Rand entities."

Tory shrugged, "The next step is we get the crystal back off Cutler, right?" she replied, before adding, "after I tear his throat out."

Morphus frowned. "The latter element is unnecessary, though it would not affect the outcome of our present undertaking," it said, with a coldness only Tory could match. "However, we must consider the possibility that the crystal is lost, or cannot be retrieved."

Hudson stood up and brushed the loose grass from his pants. His face still felt hot, and he tried to ignore it, but he couldn't shake Tory's 'pre-coital' comment from his head. "If we can't retrieve the crystal then what else can we do?" he asked, realizing he'd never even considered the possibility they might not get it back. "I thought you said they were all destroyed?"

"That is correct," replied Morphus, "but in the same way Goliath has repaired its crystal, there is a way to recombine a crystal from fragments that may still be found on the crashed Revocaters."

"How?" asked Hudson, but then another thought popped into his mind, distracting him from their current conversation. "Wait, if you're here then who's watching over Liberty's augmentation?"

"The modifications to the Liberty Devan entity are complete," Morphus replied pointing to its ship. Hudson then saw Liberty and Tobin approaching. "The augmentation was successful."

Hudson watched as Liberty got closer, noticing that her hands seemed to be shimmering. It reminded him of how Morphus looked, when it transformed into its more fluid-like form.

"Will she be okay?" asked Hudson, "She's... kinda glowing."

"She will be fine," replied Morphus, with a stillness that made Hudson feel more assured.

"Seems like you got the party started without us," said Tobin, pointing to the beer cooler. "Mind if I grab one?" he added, walking around the rocks and helping himself. He popped the cap off, gave the bottle to Liberty, then grabbed another for himself.

"So, when do we all head out?" asked Liberty, before raising the bottle to her lips. She was then momentarily distracted by the soft, iridescent glow emanating from the skin on her hands.

Morphus thought for a moment, then said, "There are still matters I need to discuss with the

Hudson Powell and Tory Bellona entities, but I interrupted them. We must let them complete their sexual coupling first."

Liberty spat out the beer in a wide spray and coughed harshly, thumping her chest. "Their what!?" she cried out.

"Severed coupling!" Hudson blurted out, "Morphus said we need to complete some repairs to a severed coupling."

Liberty frowned and glanced at Tobin, who was clearly trying his hardest to keep a straight face, but failing miserably.

"Yes, let's go and sort out that coupling," said Tory, turning and walking towards the Orion, before shooting a quick glance back at Hudson.

Hudson's eyebrows hit his hairline. Then he jabbed a thumb in the direction of Tory, and started to slink away after her. "I'd, erm, better go and give her a hand."

Liberty scowled again, looking utterly confused by Hudson's odd behavior, but then she shrugged, and said, "Fine, I'll help."

Liberty took a step towards Hudson, but Tobin was quick to intervene. "I think you need to rest after the augmentation, isn't that right Morphus? I'm sure they can handle it on their own."

Morphus also frowned, while trying to judge the meaning of the many facial expressions, mouthed words, and head shakes that Tobin was shooting in its direction, unseen by Liberty. Eventually, the alien seemed to comprehend.

"That is correct, Liberty Devan entity," said Morphus, sounding even more artificial than usual. "It is important that you rest. The Hudson Powell and Tory Bellona entities can manage this coupling by themselves."

Liberty's scowl deepened, and there was a momentary silence, before Tobin suddenly burst out into fits of giggles.

CHAPTER 23

Alien drones from Morphus' vessel buzzed around the Orion like bees around a hive. They had been working for the last hour to retrofit the VCX-110 with additional enhancements to its propulsion systems, armor and weapons. It still looked like the Orion on the outside but, bit by bit, the ship that Liberty had rebuilt in Swinsler's shipyard on Earth was becoming something else.

It was a transformation not unlike his own, Hudson mused, as he watched the drones working. On the outside, he looked the same and still wore the same clothes. This included Ericka's leather jacket, with the bullet hole in the chest, which served as a constant reminder of his journey. Yet on the inside, Hudson had changed and grown more in the last year than in the last decade. He'd gone from a gigging, freelance courier runner, lost and directionless, to a disgraced RGF cop, to a relic hunter. That would be dramatic enough on its own, but events had conspired to throw him into the center of a galactic conflict. Somehow, he was now allied with an alien AI on a mission that could decide the fate of the entire human race.

His father's words echoed in his mind again: 'Son, I wish you'd do something that you actually gave two shits about. It doesn't matter what it is, just make sure it matters to you, okay?' Hudson laughed, wondering what his father would make of him now. However, he had also come to realize something important; it wasn't what he was doing that mattered to him – it was who he was with. Liberty was family. Tobin was like the kid who was trying way too hard to impress her, but had a good heart. And Tory? He wasn't sure yet what she would do, assuming they could take down Goliath. All he knew is that he wanted her to stay.

Morphus walked up behind Hudson and held out a datapad. Hudson took it, noticing it was one from his ship, but that it had also been 'augmented', to use Morphus' own language.

"I have created a map of the Revocater and stored it in this device," Morphus said, also turning to watch the drones work. "Do you wish to go over the plan one more time?"

Hudson switched on the datapad and marveled at the intricate detail of the model Morphus had created. "Thanks, but no. I think it's all pretty clear," he replied, noticing that a small section of the Revocater had been highlighted in red. "Is this the part of the ship we need to reach?" he added, zooming in on the area in question.

"Yes," Morphus replied, without actually looking at the datapad. "That is where you will find whatever remains of the Revocater pilot, and the crystal recombiner."

The crystal recombiner was the name Morphus had made up for the device they needed, assuming they failed to recover the original crystal. Installed into the prototype Revocater, it would allow for a new crystal to be fabricated from a sufficient quantity of fragments.

Tory walked down the rear cargo ramp of the Orion and moved to Hudson's side. "I've never seen that part of the ship before," she said, studying the diagram. "That section was always either collapsed, or the corridors were too narrow to get down, even for remotes."

Morphus held out its hand, which suddenly shimmered and became molten. A few seconds later, it had returned to normal, but resting in the alien's palm was a spherical metal object.

"That's a neat trick," said Tory, as Morphus handed the object to Hudson.

The navigation hub of the Revocater was sealed off from the rest of the vessel in order to protect it from direct bombardment," Morphus said. "Our ability to alter our form allowed the pilots to enter. For you to reach the chamber, you will need this."

"What does it do?" Hudson asked, turning the object over in his hands. It looked like a small, shiny cannonball, with a thin trench running along the diameter. Hudson tried twisting it and suddenly the trench lit up red. Morphus quickly plucked the object out of Hudson's hands, and twisted it back so that the light went out.

"Unless you wish to vaporize yourself, I would suggest not doing that until it is needed," said Morphus, in a way that almost came across as scolding. It then handed the device to Tory instead.

"Wait, this is a bomb?" exclaimed Hudson.

Morphus cocked its head to one side, "It would be more accurately described as a short-range matter demolecularizer," it said, casually. "But 'bomb' will suffice."

"You could have warned me..." said Hudson, feeling like he'd lost one of his nine lives.

Morphus cocked its head to the other side, "I believe I just did?" Then before Hudson could complain again, it added, "If you roll this into one of the conduits leading into the navigation hub, it will disintegrate enough matter to allow your corporeal frames to enter."

"Blowing holes in stuff is one of my specialties," said Tory, before smiling at Hudson. "Maybe you should let me take care of the matter demolecular-thing," she said.

Hudson didn't argue; he was just glad the object was no longer glowing. "So, where do we meet you, assuming we either get the crystal back, or find this combiner thing?" Morphus didn't answer; it was staring into the sky and appeared distracted. "Morphus?" Hudson tried again, but then the alien suddenly stiffened and met his eyes.

"Goliath has arrived in this system," it said, with a coolness that did not match the enormity of the statement. "We are running out of time."

CHAPTER 24

Morphus' sudden statement felt like a hammer blow to Hudson's skull. He spun around, instinctively peering up into the sky, trying to spot the great ship. "Goliath is here, at Sapphire Alpha?" he said, scanning the horizon, but he could not see the monstrous vessel.

"Yes, and we must leave, now," Morphus said. "Goliath will destroy this planet, and its seed drones will hunt down and destroy any remaining vessels. The great ship will then continue to destroy what you call the outer portal worlds. But once Goliath detects the Revocater, it will move directly for Earth, destroying any inhabited planet in its path."

Hudson forced down a dry swallow, then said, "In that case, we should aim to meet up back at Earth. Assuming it's still there when we eventually arrive."

"Once the Revocater is activated, we will have around twenty-four of your Earth hours before Goliath arrives at System 5118208," said Morphus.

"But that's no time at all," said Hudson, throwing his arms out wide. "We can't just portal from place to place, like Goliath can."

"The modifications I made to the Orion will moderate some of the debilitating effects of high-g acceleration on your corporeal frames," replied Morphus. "This will allow you to transit between planets in far less time than would normally be possible." Then the alien entity paused and added, "Nevertheless, I would strongly suggest finding the crystal as soon as possible."

"That's the understatement of the millennium," said Hudson, but then he saw Liberty and Tobin running towards them. Liberty's skin was glowing softly, like it was covered in a light dusting of glitter.

"Something's wrong!" Liberty called out, sliding to a stop in front of them. She was staring at her glowing hands, as if they were about to explode.

"Do not be concerned, Liberty Devan entity," said Morphus, taking on a more comforting tone. "Your augmentations are merely reacting to the danger of Goliath's arrival."

"Goliath's arrival?" repeated Liberty, and then she peered up into the sky, eyes wide, just as Hudson had. "Oh, I think we should definitely be concerned!"

Hudson spun around and he saw it too. Goliath was now visible in the sky, and already appeared larger than Sapphire Alpha's small moon. He glanced at Tory, and she understood his intentions at once.

"I'll get the engines started," Tory said, before sprinting towards the Orion.

Hudson raced over to Liberty and held her shoulders gently. "I've only just gotten used to having you back," he said, realizing they were again about to be separated. "But I'll see you at Earth, okay?"

Liberty nodded, and smiled, nervously, "I'll be there; don't be late...". Then they embraced, as the ground beneath them began to shake.

"We must depart," said Morphus, "the planet's core is being removed as we speak." There was urgency even in the alien's voice now. Whether it was added for effect, or Morphus was genuinely feeling the pressure, Hudson didn't know, but it had the desired effect of motivating him to make haste.

Hudson and Liberty separated, holding each other's eyes for a second longer, and then Hudson ran for the Orion. Glancing back, he saw Tobin, Liberty and Morphus racing in the opposite direction, towards the alien shuttle. He charged up into the cargo hold and slammed the button to close the ramp. He was running so fast, he ricocheted off the corridor walls as he moved through the Orion, until he reached the cockpit. The whir of the engines had already reached a crescendo.

Tory was leaning over the secondary console, activating the new weapons systems. "We're ready to leave," she said, turning back to the pilot's chair, but Hudson was standing in front of it. Tory folded her arms and raised her eyebrows at him. "You're in my way."

Hudson held his ground, and thought he might feel more afraid about confronting Tory than he was of the giant killer spaceship in orbit. "Look, we need to talk about who does the flying," said Hudson, feeling Tory's eyes drilling into him.

"Really?" said Tory, her eyebrows raising even higher up her forehead. "The planet is about to be torn apart, and you want to do this now?"

Hudson admitted to himself that he could probably have picked a better moment, but if he didn't stake his claim now, he never would. "I've been flying since I was a kid, and I'm a good pilot," Hudson continued. "And I know this ship better than you do."

Tory's eyes narrowed slightly, as the Orion was rocked by another shudder. "Fine," she said, unfolding her arms. "But if this is going to work between us, we share the flying, agreed?"

Hudson smiled, "There's an us?"

Tory rolled her eyes and then shoved Hudson down into the pilot's seat. "Do you think you can fly us off this planet before it blows up?" she said, slipping down into the second seat and fastening her harness. Then she aimed a finger at Hudson, like it was her revolver. "But if you crash this thing, I'll break your arms."

"I'll bear that in mind," said Hudson, fastening his own harness, then quickly lifting the Orion off the slowly crumbling soil beneath them. He was fairly sure Tory was joking, but there was enough doubt at the back of his mind to make him focus on the controls even more attentively than usual.

Hudson pushed the throttle forward and the Orion shot upwards. The acceleration was ferocious and took Hudson completely by surprise, forcing him to pull back on the throttle lever. "Damn, whatever Morphus did to the engines really worked," he said, checking on Tory. However, Tory was anxiously looking at her navigation scanner.

"We have incoming," said Tory, glancing across to Hudson. "Seed ships..."

Hudson checked his own scanner display, as the blackness of space enveloped the cockpit. He turned them towards the portal, noting how the ship responded near-instantly, almost like they were still flying in Sapphire Alpha's atmosphere. Morphus had said the modifications to the Orion would enhance its maneuverability in a vacuum, but he was still surprised by how responsive the vessel was.

"Four seed ships, closing in fast," said Hudson, "I think we're going to need to test out these new augmented weapons."

He glanced across to Tory, but she was already on it. The targeting overlay was displayed on the cockpit glass, and the new dorsal and ventral cannons were already tracking the incoming targets. Hudson spun the ship around and rotated the engine pods, so that they were facing the oncoming ships. But it was the imposing sight of Goliath that stole his attention.

They both watched in rapt silence as Goliath continued its apocalyptic assault. Just as had occurred at Chrome One, a purple vortex began to swell on the opposite side of the planet to where Goliath hung in orbit. Seconds later the core matter was expelled into space and the portal snapped shut, leaving a void in the center of the planet. A void that was instantly filled by the violent collapse of the outer core. The planet began to break up in front of Hudson's eyes, and Goliath turned, lining up the next destination for its voyage of destruction.

"If you're going to insist on flying, then can you actually fly?!" Tory called out, jolting Hudson back to the moment. He checked the navigation scanner, and stood ready on their physics-defying thrusters to evade the oncoming seed ships. He knew that Morphus had also upgraded the Orion's armor, but he didn't want to chance that it could take a head-on hit from the arrow-like seed ships.

"I'll be ready," Hudson called back. "It would be nice if you took out one or two before they got here though..."

Tory squeezed the trigger and fierce red bolts of energy sped out in front of the Orion, taking them both by surprise. A second later there were two explosions, and two of the seed ships disappeared off Hudson's navigation scanner.

"Show off," said Hudson, as he pulsed the thrusters to dodge the remaining two ships. The Orion responded with a rapidity that should have left them as stains on the wall, and the seed ships raced past. Reverting the engine pods to their standard configuration, Hudson targeted one of the remaining two ships and accelerated after it. The arrow-like vessel spun back towards them, but Tory was already waiting on the trigger. She fired volleys from both cannons, again sending bolts of energy searing out into space, and the ship was engulfed in flames.

"I could get used to these," said Tory, clearly enjoying herself, but then the Orion was hit, and sent into a spin.

Hudson wrestled with the controls to counteract their motion, while anxiously glancing at the damage control panel. Remarkably, there were no red lights showing.

"No damage," Tory called out, "Apart from us maybe needing to hammer out a ding in the hull."

Hudson regained control, then focused on the final blip on the scanner. However, then he noticed dozens more seed ships approaching. "I think that will do for a shake-down test of the new systems," he said, turning back towards the portal, and accelerating harder. He could see that Morphus' was already at the threshold. "We'll have to let this last one go." There was another flash of red light and another explosion, and Hudson saw the last of the four seed ships vanish off the scanner.

"It's already gone..." said Tory, coolly.

"Now you really are showing off..." said Hudson, though not for the first time, he was glad of Tory's expert aim.

Hudson saw the portal flash open ahead of them, then Morphus' ship also disappeared off the scanners. He waited until the last moment, then spun the Orion around and decelerated hard. He realized the ship must have been pushing ten or fifteen g-forces, but even with the alien tech that Morphus had infused into the Orion's DNA, the pressure on their bodies was still immense.

"Ten seconds..." Hudson called out, watching the second wave of seed ships close in. The Orion began to vibrate, shaking them even harder than the quakes on the planet had done.

"Five seconds!" Hudson shouted. Then he cut the deceleration burn, spun them around, and pulsed the thrusters to realign them with the portal.

"Transiting now!" There was a bright flash of purple light, and the forces on their bodies were gone. He looked to Tory and she was staring back at him. To his surprise, she was smiling.

Then there was another bright flash, and they were pressed into their seats for a second time, as the Orion emerged into normal space again. They were through, and safe for now, but Hudson knew they had escaped one danger only to fly willingly towards another. Hudson reached over to the navigation scanner and updated their course to lock in the next waypoint. Their destination was the Gale Basin, on Mars. And, perhaps, a final rendezvous with Cutler Wendell and Logan Griff.

CHAPTER 25

Griff and Cutler sat in stunned silence as their debilitated shuttle finally approached Earth. However, it wasn't the sight of the blue planet that had awed them. Waiting in orbit was an armada of CET warships, the likes of which hadn't been seen since the early days of the Earth-Mars war. They ranged from powerful capital ships, the size of luxury cruise liners, to small, two-man armored shuttles, and everything in-between.

"How many are there?" asked Cutler, steering a course that took them as far from the bulk of the fleet as possible.

Griff slapped his palm on the side of the navigation scanner, causing the image to jolt and wobble. "Hell, I don't know," he grumbled, "Nothing on this piece of shit shuttle works." Then the image stabilized for a moment; it was long enough for Griff to get a reasonable impression of the fleet's size. "There's got to be three hundred ships, maybe more. That's most of the damned fleet!"

A whiny alarm sounded and Cutler quickly silenced it, before checking his instruments. "We have experienced another drop in fuel pressure, and number two engine is faltering. There are also failures in the magnetic field coils and a slight radiation leak."

It was the last part that got Griff's attention, "A radiation leak?" he said, turning his attention away from the fleet. "Just how slight are we talking?"

Cutler studied the data for a second, before replying, "It is not dangerous yet, but we must set down soon."

Cutler's dry delivery didn't help to instill Griff with confidence, but the looming threat did work to focus his mind on the task at hand. He rapidly cycled through the communications menu on his console, until he found the RGF control tower at Hunter's Point in San Francisco. "I'm requesting clearance to land at an RGF base," he explained to Cutler as he worked. "If we dock at a regular spaceport, the biometric ID scanners will identify us the moment we step off the ship."

"Hunter's point is close to Swinsler's Shipyard," replied Cutler, appearing to be satisfied with Griff's choice of port. "There is a refuge there that will suffice."

"Anywhere is better than this broken-down tin can," replied Griff, glowering at the stained upholstery of his chair. "For once, I actually can't wait to set foot back on Earth."

"That may be more challenging than we first thought," replied Cutler. "It appears that the CET has revoked the RGF's independent authority, and has taken the force under its control."

"What?" snapped Griff. "Are you sure?" He'd heard Cutler clearly enough, but didn't believe it. He switched his monitor to a local news feed, and cycled through the bulletins. It didn't take long to confirm what Cutler had said. "They've suspended all of the top leadership, and halted all relic hunting operations, until the alien threat is dealt with," said Griff, reading one of the more detailed articles. "But since the CET military is pre-occupied up here, I doubt they'll be paying that much attention to what goes on in the bases. We might get lucky."

Cutler continued to pilot the ship towards Earth, aiming for a re-entry slot that would bring them in along the west coast of North America. The communications panel then lit up, and Griff checked it, expecting it to be a reply from Hunter's Point. However, to Griff's dismay, the request turned out to be from one of the CET cruisers.

"Don't answer it," said Griff, noticing Cutler's hand sliding over to the panel. "Pretend we have a comms issue or something."

Cutler hovered his hand over the switch. "They will simply block our path and communicate with signal lights instead," he replied. "You RGF types may be used to ignoring the CET's authority, but you're the same as the rest of us now."

Griff scowled. It was often difficult to read Cutler's emotions, because of his dull intonations. However, this time he could clearly hear the satisfaction in Cutler's voice while he was reminding Griff of his newly-reduced status. "Authority or not, we can't let them stop us," said Griff. "It won't take them long to realize something doesn't add up with our ship."

"I will stall them," replied Cutler, adjusting his headset mic so that it was closer to his mouth. "But if you cannot get clearance from the RGF, we are caught anyway. Whether in orbit or on the ground, the CET will have us."

Griff growled and returned to his communication panel, while Cutler flipped open the channel to the CET cruiser.

"Unidentified shuttle, this is Commander Lane of the CET Light Cruiser Humboldt," the CET officer began, his voice crackly and indistinct through the shuttle's glitchy comms system. "We are detecting a radiation leak from your engines. And your transponder ID is not active. Do you require assistance?"

Cutler took a deep breath and answered, putting on a fake accent and feigning cheerfulness.

"Cruiser Humboldt, this is Shuttle Logan, thanks for your concern," Cutler began. Griff found Cutler's put-on sunniness disconcerting. "We hit some space junk coming out of the portal, but we're doing just fine. We'll be setting down at Ride Spaceport for repairs ASAP."

There was a short pause, during which time Griff said, "Shuttle Logan? You couldn't have thought of something else?" But Cutler just glared back at him and waited.

The voice of Commander Lane crackled over the speakers again, "Understood Shuttle Logan," Transmit your entry clearance and we'll let you be on your way."

Cutler muted the link and turned to Griff. "This is where you finally prove your usefulness, Inspector," he said. Although he had resumed his normal, flat speaking voice, Griff could still detect an undertone of aggression. Turning the mic back on, Cutler replied to the cruiser, "Will do, Commander. Give us a minute or two to pull it up. We're still a little glitchy over here."

"Understood, Shuttle Logan, standing by," came the reply, and the link clicked off.

Griff knew they had already had some luck with the CET cruiser. Ordinarily, a CET commander on patrol would be bored enough, and pedantic enough, to stop and search a wreck of a shuttle like theirs. However, the CET were clearly too concerned with other matters to be bothered with them.

Then Griff's message indicator lit up, and the response came back from the RGF base at Hunter's Point. Griff read it and swore, "Shit, the base has been closed to all traffic in and out until further notice," he said. Then he had an idea, and quickly opened a new data connection on his panel. "I'm going to see if my security codes still work."

Cutler glanced across to him, "What will that achieve?"

Griff established the link and then started to log-in. "I was essentially working undercover for Wash," replied Griff. "Which meant I could move in and out of RGF facilities off the books. If I can get access, and my codes still work, I might be able to grant us clearance directly." Then he noticed that Cutler appeared to have stopped listening, and was hurriedly entering a new entry program into the computer. "What are you doing?" Griff asked, scowling across to him.

"If you fail, then clearly, we cannot submit to the CET authorities," replied Cutler calmly. "So, we will have no choice but to enter the atmosphere without clearance."

Griff spun his seat around to face the mercenary, "That's suicide!" he yelled. "They'll either destroy us before we reach the atmosphere, or shoot us down as soon as we make it through!"

The message panel on Cutler's console lit up. It was an incoming communication request from the CET cruiser. It had clearly run out of patience with them.

Cutler grabbed the controls and placed his hand on the thruster lever, before glancing back at Griff. "Then you had better get clearance quickly," he replied, coolly. "You have sixty seconds, before that cruiser decides we're a threat, and disables our engines."

Griff shook his head and spun back to face his console. He used his credentials to connect to the RGF computer systems, but the data was loading slowly. "Damn this piece of crap!" he growled, again slapping the monitor on the side. "The link is too slow; you have to give me more time!"

"You have forty seconds..." Cutler replied, flatly.

Griff slapped the monitor again, and the RGF data portal finally loaded. He checked his access level and shook his fist triumphantly. "I still have clearance," he called over, "I'm authorizing us for an emergency landing."

"Twenty seconds, Inspector..." said Cutler.

"Damn it, just wait another minute!" Griff snarled back, as he focused on the screen. *Come on, process already!* he urged, as the cursor continued to blink silently.

"Ten seconds, before we have to run..." said Cutler, tightening his grip on the thruster lever.

Griff's screen updated with the clearance code. "I have it!" Griff shouted, turning the monitor so that Cutler could read it. "Call back the damn cruiser!"

Cutler glanced at the monitor, before taking his hand off the thruster control. "It's about time you were useful," he said, with a rare acidity to his delivery, before flipping open the channel to the cruiser. Griff felt his face redden with anger, but he had to bite his tongue, while Cutler spoke to Commander Lane again.

"My most sincere apologies, Commander Lane," Cutler began, putting on his fake voice again. It just made Griff want to punch him even harder. "We had a few additional technical difficulties to iron out, but I'm transmitting the entry clearance now."

They waited, while the channel remained open to the cruiser. Static crackled over the speakers, like a turntable, playing the lead-in track to an old and worn LP.

Shit! It's taking too long... Griff thought to himself. He began running scenarios in his mind. If Cutler ran, they'd be destroyed for sure. However, perhaps he could turn in Cutler, and claim he had been captured by the mercenary. *It would be an RGF Inspector's word over that of a suspected criminal,* he reasoned to himself. It was a long shot, but it was better than burning up in the Earth's atmosphere.

Griff slid his fingers slowly onto his holster, and gently teased open the strap holding his pistol in place. Checking to make sure Cutler wasn't watching, he then closed his hand around the grip, and began to slowly draw the weapon. Suddenly, Commander Lane's voice crackled through the cockpit speakers again.

"Apologies for the wait, Shuttle Logan," said Lane, "It's all a bit hectic up here right now. Your entry clearance has been confirmed. Make sure you get that radiation leak looked at."

Griff let out his breath slowly, realizing that he'd been holding it for the last few seconds. He then slid the weapon back into its holster, as Cutler cheerfully answered the cruiser.

"Will do, Commander, it sure is comforting to know you guys are up here," said Cutler, with a saccharin sweetness that made Griff feel nauseous. "Shuttle Logan, out."

Cutler then closed the channel, and resumed his previous entry course, before glancing across to Griff and frowning. "You look pale, Inspector," he said, derisively. "I would have expected you to handle such situations with more of a level head."

Griff felt like pulling out his weapon and shooting him right then and there, but he instead sat back. *I'll show you level-headedness...* Griff thought, as the blue planet started to fill their view outside. *Soon, I won't need you anymore. Then you'll find out how calmly I can act, when I put a bullet in your arrogant head.*

"How about you just concern yourself with landing the damn shuttle," snapped Griff, before noticing that he was still connected to the RGF data portal. He was about to shut down the window, when he spotted that he had a personal communication. Frowning, he turned the monitor away from Cutler so that he couldn't see it, and opened the message. His eyes widened as he saw who it was from, but he was careful not to let Cutler see his shocked expression.

It read: 'From: Superintendent Jane Wash [Suspended]. Subject: Mutual benefit.' Griff cast a surreptitious glance across to Cutler again, but the mercenary was completely consumed by the task of re-entry, and was paying no attention to Griff. He continued reading. 'As I'm sure you now know, the RGF is finished. I have been suspended, pending an investigation by a joint CET and MP board. It's a formality – they intend to make an example of me, but I won't let that happen. You created this damned mess, so you will help get me out of it, or I swear I will take you down with me. You know I will! But, since I know what truly motivates you, I will point out that I am still a very rich woman. Help me to acquire a counterfeit ID and get me away from the core planets, and I'll make you a rich man. I know – and you know – you won't get a better offer, even if you rat on me to these CET assholes. Which I'm sure you're considering even now. I KNOW you, Griff! Reply here with your answer. Wash.'

Griff smiled, but then quickly wiped the grin from his face, afraid that Cutler might see it and suspect something. Luckily, the mercenary was still too distracted. Griff thought that turning over Cutler and what he knew about Wash was his best option, but Wash had just gifted him another. Wash was right that even if he did dish the dirt on her, there were no guarantees the CET authorities would be lenient with him. However, with Wash's money, he could not only get a fake ID for her, but for himself too. And the thought of taking back the credits that the witch had extorted out of him over the years was too tempting to ignore.

A smile again curled his lips, as he hit 'reply' and typed out a simple, short response. 'I agree to your proposal. Meet me at Swinsler's Shipyard, Hunter's Point, San Francisco.' He transmitted the message, waited for it to send, then closed down the RGF data portal.

"We'll be on the ground within the hour," said Cutler, as flames started to encroach on their view of the planet. "I've laid low at Swinsler's lot before. We can get this shuttle fixed up there too."

"Sure, whatever," said Griff, playing with the strap on his holster. "Sounds like a plan." Then he glanced across to Cutler again, and smiled. He'd gotten rid of Tory Bellona, and soon the problem of Cutler Wendell would be dealt with too. *Swinsler's shipyard is where you'll lay low, alright.* he thought. *Low, as in buried six-feet in the ground...*

CHAPTER 26

The smile on Liberty's face grew wider, as she turned for another pass around the asteroid. She was now fully in control of Morphus' shuttle for the first time. The alien AI had yielded all controls to her as a test, and she was passing with flying colors.

Morphus had recreated a replica of the VCX-110's cockpit and flight controls, as a way for Liberty to feel more comfortable flying the ship. However, despite the clear similarities in terms of the mechanical design of the control systems and instruments, the aesthetic appearance was still very 'alien'. Everything looked as if it had been cast in a mold, as a single, unified piece, rather than bolted together from many component pieces. And while Liberty still had to actually move the controls in order to pilot the vessel, the connection between pilot and ship was more than merely physical. She was also connected to it via her new alien augmentations, which interfaced directly with Liberty's central nervous system. Morphus had explained it as a being a symbiosis of organic and inorganic components. It sounded impossible, yet it worked.

Tobin drew his hands away from his face for the third time in the last minute, as Liberty veered back out into deep space again. Her initial flight training may have been a thrill-ride for Liberty, but for Tobin it had been the roller-coaster ride from hell. He sucked in another gulp of air and exhaled slowly, before anxiously turning to Morphus, who was standing between their two seats.

"Remind me again how the ship can move like this, without us being squished against the walls?" said Tobin. He'd asked Morphus the question once before already. However, it had been during one of Liberty's earlier sprints over the asteroid, and he'd been too pre-occupied with an impending, fiery death to hear the answer.

"This vessel is capable of manipulating the curvature of spacetime," replied Morphus, as casually as if it were describing something as simple as a door hinge. The alien entity's hands were pressed behind its back, like an eighteenth-century naval commander. "But within a planetary atmosphere, it can also use what you would consider to be more conventional reaction-based thruster technology."

"Right..." said Tobin, who then glanced at Liberty, clearly not having understood a word of what Morphus said.

Liberty shrugged, momentarily taking her shimmering hands off the controls, which just had the effect of making Tobin look more nervous. "Right now, I don't care how it works," she said, grabbing the controls again, before dipping back towards the asteroid's rocky surface. "But I like it!"

Tobin shook his head, but then covered his eyes again as Liberty dove into a deep crater, before powering up the slope on the other side.

"We should continue on through the portal," said Morphus, in its usual, composed manner. "Your abilities will be sufficient to begin your acclimatization to the Revocater's systems. I have begun the process of cortical integration in order to provide you with the necessary knowledge."

Suddenly, Liberty froze and was pressed back into her seat, with her eyes tightly closed. Tobin yelped, and went to grab the controls, before realizing that they had begun to move by themselves. The ship had already turned away from the asteroid, and was heading towards the portal.

"You could have warned me!" said Tobin, pressing a hand to his chest.

Liberty then opened her eyes and let out a labored gasp, as if she had just surfaced from a long underwater dive. "Me too!" she exclaimed. "It would be nice to have some notice before you start messing with my brain." Then Liberty's eyes widened, and she started pouting and blinking elaborately, as if she was sucking on an especially sour piece of lime.

"Are you okay?" asked Tobin, frowning at her. "You're pulling some pretty funky faces there..."

Liberty scowled at Tobin, in-between pouts and blinks. Then she shook her head and let out another long breath. "Well, that was interesting..." she said, rubbing her temples.

"I apologize, I should have warned you before implanting such a vast array of knowledge," said Morphus. "But now you should have the requisite abilities necessary to pilot the Revocater."

Tobin smiled, "Are you able to implant any knowledge into my head too?" he asked. "My mom never forgave me for flunking out of business school."

Liberty shook her head and glanced back at Morphus. "While you ponder that very important question, how long is it until we reach the Corporeal's homeworld?"

"This is the final portal transition," replied Morphus, before looking to Tobin. "And yes, Tobin Rand entity, I can assist with your knowledge, but not your academic inadequacies."

Liberty and Tobin laughed, before the view outside was consumed by a swirling purple energy. Seconds later the ship emerged back into normal space in front of a silver-colored orb, hanging in orbit above a vivid blue planet.

"Oh, wow, what is that?" wondered Liberty out loud, as she stared out at the massive metal sphere in awe. "Is that the Telescope? Hudson told me about it, from the memories you implanted in his head." However, Morphus was oddly silent. Liberty looked back at the alien, but its face – that of the human female they'd become accustomed to seeing – seemed strangely absent of life. It was as if the entity had been frozen in a moment in time. Then the lights in the artificial cockpit dimmed, and Liberty heard the thrum of the ship's mysterious power source wind down. Liberty and Tobin exchanged nervous glances, before Liberty again turned to Morphus. "Morphus, what's going on?" she asked, more urgently. "What's wrong?"

Morphus stepped closer to the viewport, which suddenly zoomed in on the massive sphere. Liberty looked out, initially seeing nothing more than the glow of the system's sun reflecting off the sphere's metal surface. And then she saw it. A dark, arrow-like shape, buzzing around the sphere like a moth around a light bulb. It was a seed ship.

"Goliath has sent its drones here," said Morphus, finally breaking its silence. Then it looked down to meet Liberty's eyes. "They must be searching for the Revocater."

The image in front of Liberty switched to show an area of the planet's surface. It was a fractured wasteland, smashed and broken from Goliath's relentless assault, millennia ago. However, unlike the first time Morphus had returned to its creator's homeworld, there was now something moving on the surface. The objects had a design similar to that of the arrow-shaped seed ships. But instead of flying, they scurried over the scarred landscape, like mechanized arachnids.

"But how does it know?" asked Tobin, tearing his eyes away from the sinister-looking drones to look at Morphus. "Goliath must be half the galaxy away from here?"

Morphus adjusted the view on the screen again, focusing on the area where the service tunnel was located. There were no seed ships or spider-like surface drones directly near it, but Liberty could see that they were getting closer.

"When I detected Goliath at the planet you call Sapphire Alpha, it must also have sensed my presence," replied Morphus. "Goliath does not know our intentions, but the great ship is wise. It will know that if a Revocater pilot survived, then it will be searching for a way to destroy it."

"But you can destroy these drones, right?" said Liberty, wondering why Morphus had appeared to power down. "You can stop them, before they find the Revocater?"

"If the seed drones and ships detect us and the Revocater, they will return to Goliath and inform it," replied Morphus. "The great ship will then make destroying me and the Revocater its top priority. And until I have the crystal, I am powerless to defeat it." Morphus stepped back, so that the entity disappeared into shadow. From the darkness, they heard its voice again. "We must reach the prototype Revocater without being detected."

Suddenly, the image switched back to the view of the Telescope over the planet, and their ship began to move. However, it was not only moving – it was reconfiguring itself too. Liberty could see bulkheads shifting and panels folding and bending. Without warning, the cockpit shrank and became suddenly claustrophobic. Liberty instinctively pressed her hands up, trying to brace the ceiling that seemed to be collapsing in on her, but she could not hold it back. She screamed and ducked, covering her head, but then the movement of the ship's surfaces stopped as suddenly as they had begun. The cockpit fell into silence.

Liberty opened her eyes and peered around. There was barely space for Liberty and Tobin, and the alien entity was nowhere to be seen

"Morphus!" Liberty cried out, feeling terror grip her. It was like she had been entombed in a metal sarcophagus and buried alive. "Morphus, where are you?!"

There was a deathly silence, punctuated by the rising beat of Liberty's heart thumping in her chest. Then the alien AI spoke.

"I am still here, Liberty Devan entity," said Morphus. "I had to act quickly to reconfigure the ship, before we were detected."

Liberty threw her head back in relief. "You scared the hell out of me!" she shouted.

"I apologize, but the expedience was necessary," replied Morphus. The unearthly thrum of the engines then increased in volume, and the ship began moving rapidly towards the planet.

"Wait, won't they see us?" asked Tobin.

"I have reconfigured this vessel so that it appears to be a seed ship," replied Morphus. "Goliath's servants are many in number, but they lack sophisticated intelligence. In many respects, they are analogous to your Earth-based wolves."

"So, you're hoping they'll just see us as another member of the pack and leave us alone?" asked Tobin.

"Correct, Tobin Rand entity," replied Morphus. "In this configuration, we will be able to reach the subterranean complex where the Revocater is located without being detected."

Liberty nodded and let her body relax, at least as much as the cramped surroundings allowed. "We really need to work on your communication skills, Morphus," she said, closing her eyes. Then she had a terrible thought, and looked up at the metal above her head, as if it were Morphus' face. "What happens if those spider-drones have already gotten inside the complex, and found the prototype Revocater?"

"Then we must fight, and destroy them, before they cripple the Revocater," said Morphus, with a cool resolve. "The Revocater must not be lost. The survival of all corporeal life depends on it."

CHAPTER 27

The journey to the surface of the Corporeals' planet was the most uncomfortable Liberty had ever experienced. This was not only because of the cramped confines of the cockpit, but because of the risk of being discovered. It felt like hiding in a school locker, while the bully patrolled the corridor outside, looking for her next victim.

Morphus had assumed full control of the ship again, as they descended steadily towards the service tunnel. Other seed ships flew by, seemingly oblivious to their true nature, while the spider-like drones crawled over the surface. However, as Morphus' ship dipped lower than the jagged remains of the smashed skyscrapers, it became apparent that the surface drones had now discovered the service tunnel too.

"Look, they're already inside," said Tobin, pointing to the image in front of him. "We're too late!"

"There is no need for concern yet, Tobin Rand entity," came the disembodied voice of Morphus. Liberty had certainly grown to appreciate the alien's naturally calm demeanor. It helped to deflate the steadily rising tensions inside the cockpit. "In order to destroy the Revocater, the drones will need to reach its reactor core, and detonate inside," Morphus continued. The ship then entered the tunnel and their tiny cockpit was thrown into near-total darkness. The only illumination came from the soft glow of Liberty's iridescent skin. "But they will first have to cut through the hull to enter. If we move quickly, they may not yet have succeeded."

Morphus reached the end of the tunnel, spun the ship around and set it down. Liberty could see the entrance to the service tunnel closing behind them.

"Won't the seed ships alert Goliath once they see us coming?" asked Liberty, as the cockpit began to expand around her. Morphus was reconfiguring the vessel back to its previous shape.

"I have interfaced with the complex's core systems and temporarily supplied it with power," said Morphus. Then the entity rose up out of the floor behind them, like a lava lamp bubbling upwards, and assumed its female form. "Until my reserves are depleted, this will allow me to seal off the complex from the surface, and jam any outgoing transmissions."

"But for how long will your reserves last?" asked Liberty.

Morphus thought for a moment and answered, "For around two of your Earth hours, then I must disconnect and replenish."

Liberty shrugged and nodded, "I guess we're on the clock, anyway, so what's another deadline to worry about?"

"Once we have secured the Revocater, I can link its power systems to the complex instead," Morphus continued. "Assuming we do not allow any of the seed drones to escape, Goliath will not detect us, until we launch."

Tobin laughed, nervously, "And how exactly are us three supposed to stop them escaping?"

Liberty raised her eyebrows and turned to Morphus. She wanted to hear the answer as much as Tobin did. Two 'corporeals' and a single alien AI, against an unknown number of vicious-looking machines the size of rhinos, didn't seem like great odds.

"I'm a terrible shot, so I won't be much help," Tobin added, continuing to point out the flaws in Morphus' plan. Then he gestured to Liberty, and added, "And while Liberty is undeniably lethal with a pair of tonfas, a couple of sticks won't do any good against those spider things."

"Tonfas; interesting..." replied Morphus, which was not the response that Liberty had expected. And judging by the bemused look on Tobin's face, it wasn't the response he was expecting either. Then Morphus turned and headed towards the rear of the compartment, which reconfigured as it approached. Liberty and Tobin exchanged further confused glances, then got out of their seats to follow the alien.

"My combat capabilities are highly advanced," said Morphus without ego, as two objects were slowly ejected out of compartments that had just appeared. "But I will still require your assistance." Turning to Liberty, it added, "In many ways, this will be no different to what you called 'hunts' on the wrecked Revocaters," and then to Tobin, it said, "or your rescue of the Tory Bellona entity."

Liberty glanced at Tobin, but Morphus' words of encouragement – if that's what they were – didn't appear to have convinced him. However, Liberty was more concerned with the contents of the compartments. Curiosity got the better of her, and she approached one, before cautiously peering inside. Then she laughed. It was mostly a laugh of surprise, but Liberty certainly also considered what she saw in the compartment to be a joke. In front of her was a pair of tonfas, fashioned from the same alien alloy that the ship seemed to be constructed from.

"You can't be serious," said Liberty, holding up one of the weapons. It had the exact weight and balance as the ones she had misappropriated from the torture room on New Providence. "I can't fight massive alien spider drones with two metal sticks!"

Morphus appeared to be entirely unconcerned by Liberty's incredulous reaction. "It is best that you fight with what you know," it said, before moving to the second compartment. "But, like your own corporeal frame, I have modified this weapon, and dramatically increased its lethality."

Liberty raised an eyebrow, and held the weapon a little further away from her body. "That doesn't sound good..." she said, scowling at the tonfa as if it might suddenly explode.

Morphus didn't respond, and instead picked up a pistol from the second chamber, before offering it to Tobin. It looked like a pretty typical nine-millimeter, except that it was cast from a single solid piece of alien metal. The only moving part appeared to be the trigger.

"Hey, I'm the last person you should be handing some alien ray gun to," said Tobin, pulling his hands away from the weapon. "I'm just as likely to shoot one of you two as I am the spider things."

Morphus was again undeterred, and held the pistol out closer. "This will ensure that you are an asset, rather than a liability," the alien said.

Tobin now folded his arms and scowled, "Now you sound just like my mom."

Morphus frowned, but continued, "To effectively use this weapon, you will require some minor augmentations to the musculoskeletal structure of your arm, and a small modification to your brain."

Tobin's scowl remained, "A *what* now?"

Liberty laughed, and cut-in, "You'll get a bit of glowy skin, like me, that's all. No big deal."

Tobin shook his head, "Fine, it's not like I'm going to stay here on this creepy ship all by myself," he said, taking the weapon. "How does it work, anywaaaaaaaaaay!" His final word turned into a scream, as a part of the weapon's frame became amorphous and wrapped around his wrist. "What is it doing to me?!" he yelled, shaking his arm as if he was trying to dislodge a snake that had coiled around it. Then he stopped suddenly and froze. He squeezed his eyes shut a few times, like he was trying to blink some grit out of them, then shook his head vigorously. After a couple of seconds, he stopped, and appeared to act normally again. Tobin glanced warily at Morphus, then turned to Liberty. "Well, that was just about the weirdest thing I've ever experienced..." he said.

"Do you now comprehend how to use this weapon?" asked Morphus.

Tobin shrugged and then said, "That's the weird thing; I don't know how, but I do."

"Good, then one final thing before we proceed," said Morphus, returning to the compartments. It then picked up and held out two jackets. Liberty's appeared exactly the same as the relic hunter jacket she'd bought on Brahms Three, minus some of the holes and patches. Similarly, Tobin's looked like a replica of the off-white Nehru fashion jacket he was already wearing.

"They look the same as what we already have on. So, what gives?" asked Liberty, taking the jacket from Morphus' hand. However, although it looked the same, Liberty immediately realized it felt completely different. It was heavier, and as she examined it under the vessel's vivid white light, it also appeared to shimmer.

"I have fabricated these with high-density fibers that will help to protect your fragile corporeal torsos and internal organs," answered Morphus.

Liberty took off her jacket, and began to transfer the contents of her pockets to the new garment. This included the remaining few hundred hardbucks that she'd previously stored in her quarters on the Orion. She caught Tobin shaking his head at her. "Don't look at me like that!" she snapped at him, "There are a lot of bars where you can only get a drink if you have hardbucks. And since that asshole, Werner, stole most of my stash on New Providence, I'm not letting these notes out of my sight."

"Nice to see you have your priorities straight," said Tobin, with a cheeky smile. Then he removed his jacket and pulled on the one that Morphus had given him. Liberty caught him checking out how he looked in the polished reflective surface of the ship's walls, and smiled.

"Shouldn't we have the same protection for the lower half too?" asked Tobin, pointing to his designer pants.

"I have no more resources to spare at this time," said Morphus. "Though you could still survive the loss of a leg, if treated quickly enough. Your vital organs are more challenging to repair."

Coming from anyone else, Liberty would have assumed this to have been an attempt at humor. However, coming from Morphus, she knew the alien entity was probably serious. She glanced across to Tobin, who appeared positively horrified.

"And what about our heads?" asked Tobin. "Do you have any resources spare to help protect our squidgy corporeal brains?"

"I do not," replied Morphus, but the entity then appeared to consider this question in more detail, before adding, "I advise that you do not get hit in the head."

Liberty and Tobin's mouths fell open. "Please tell me that's your idea of a joke?" said Liberty, hoping more than ever that the alien's study of humanity had extended to satire.

Morphus considered this for a moment. "No, it is my idea of advice," then it laughed stiffly, and added, "but yes, I can see how you may consider it to be darkly humorous."

Liberty shook her head. "We really, really need to work on your communication skills."

"And your sense of humor..." Tobin added.

Morphus shot them a confused frown, then turned to face the wall, before pressing a hand to the smooth surface. The ship reconfigured and a ramp lowered on to the deck outside. Lights flickered on, illuminating a perfect, sheer metal wall, built into the rock.

Morphus glanced back at them both. "Are you ready, Liberty Devan and Tobin Rand entities?"

Liberty shook her head, "Absolutely not." She then picked up the strange alien tonfas and stepped beside Morphus. "But one way or another, this is going to be one hell of a last relic hunt."

CHAPTER 28

Morphus led them inside the shipyard complex, still in its human female form. Some of the doors had already been forced open, and there were scratch marks in the floor and walls. Liberty knelt down and ran her hand along one of the scratches; the cut was deep and clean.

"What could have cut so deeply into metal this thick?" asked Liberty. Though she had a worrying suspicion that it was the result of the scythe-like legs of the seed drones.

"The seed drones were originally designed to help reform the landscapes on planets targeted for corporeal life," said Morphus. "However, their tools also make for formidable weapons."

"I think it's better if we stop asking questions like that..." Tobin cut in, "because I get the feeling we're never going to like the answers."

"I will deal with any seed drones attempting to breach the Revocater's hull," said Morphus, as it advanced in the lead, barely making a sound.

"And what do we do?" asked Liberty, following on, and jumping at every little noise that filtered along the wide corridor, no matter how faint or distant.

"The seed drones will focus their attacks on me," said Morphus. "The more you can destroy and prevent from attacking me, the greater our chances of success. Even a single seed drone detonating inside the reactor core would ensure the vessel is too damaged to operate. And alone, I have no hope of repairing it, before Goliath finishes it's task."

Liberty nodded, but wondered why Morphus had not changed its shape. "Wouldn't you have more success fighting these drones if you morphed into a form that was a bit more..." she hesitated, searching for the right word, before settling on, "aggressive?"

Morphus led them into a corridor that did not appear to have any scratches or signs that the seed drones had been there. "I have grown accustomed to this form," it said, forcing open another door.

"Sure, but human bodies are not well-suited to hand-fighting giant metal spider drones," replied Liberty, following Morphus through the door. Liberty thought that if she had the ability to morph into something more capable of fending off the drones, she would do, and was curious as to why Morphus had not. Then, worrying whether her comment might upset Morphus, she added, "No offence... I like your current form. It's just perhaps not the best one right now."

"No offence taken, Liberty Devan entity," said Morphus, coolly. "However, if I were to adopt another form, I would no longer be Morphus."

This stopped Liberty in her tracks, and she huffed a surprised laugh. She hadn't thought that Morphus considered its new form to be part of its identity, rather than something adopted merely to make it easier for humans to accept it. However, now she thought about it, what Morphus had said made perfect sense.

"But please be assured that this form will not hinder my combat effectiveness," Morphus added.

Liberty remained unconvinced that two arms and two legs would be any use fighting the spider-like drones, but didn't question Morphus any further. The fact that the shape-shifting alien had become attached to this one form made it seem more real, somehow.

Morphus then led them up onto a higher level, but the path ahead was blocked by a massive metal double door. It looked like the sort of door that could withstand the blast of a rocket taking off. To Liberty's total astonishment, Morphus stepped up to the metal slabs and forced them open as easily as if it were a Japanese shoji sliding door. It was a herculean feat of strength that left Liberty dumbstruck.

"I think that answers your question about Morphus' capabilities..." said Tobin, smiling, as he brushed past her.

The corridor widened into what appeared to be a large viewing gallery. The glass wall had been smashed through in several places, and a cold breeze swept in through the holes. And in the cavernous space beyond this, Liberty could see the unmistakable shape of an alien hulk; a Revocater. However, unlike every other vessel of its kind that she'd seen before, this one was not smashed and broken, and it wasn't weathered by centuries of rain and dust. Despite the fact it was likely tens or even hundreds of thousands of years old, it looked brand new.

Morphus peered around the room, then pointed to a large archway on the far wall. To Liberty's surprise, it opened into another space, which seemed to have no other exits. The alien turned to them; the expression on its human female face was suddenly grave and serious.

"Tobin Rand entity, you can engage the seed drones that attack me from this vantage point," said Morphus. Then it turned to Liberty and added, "While you, Liberty Devan entity, must defend our corporeal male ally, and ensure that he can complete his task."

Tobin glanced out through the smashed glass, again looking highly dubious of his role. "Even with these augmentations, are you sure I can hit anything from this range?"

"Trust yourself," replied Morphus, "and your aim will be true." Then it pointed to the room through the archway on the far wall. "But, as I believe you human corporeals say, 'do not be a hero'," Morphus continued. "I cannot pilot the Revocater alone. If the seed drones come for you, run to this room and seal the door. There is a button on the wall to the right as you enter. Seal yourself inside and wait for me to return."

Liberty nodded, but then spoke with a matching seriousness, "Agreed, but you're not indestructible either, Morphus. And you sure as hell aren't expendable. We need you in one piece too."

Morphus cocked its head to one side, "Technically, I am not formed from individual pieces," it answered, prompting Liberty to raise a weary eyebrow. Then, to Liberty's surprise, Morphus offered a smile, "But, I understand your meaning."

"Good luck," said Liberty, placing both hands squarely on the alien's shoulders, which felt like lumps of solid rubber. "To all of us..."

Morphus nodded and moved to one of the shattered holes in the window. Tobin and Liberty crept to the other side, and crouched low. From her new vantage, Liberty could now clearly see the spider-like seed drones on the hull of the Revocater. They were positioned directly in line with them, roughly a quarter of the way up from the ship's massive engines. Liberty counted eight drones, and they were cutting into the hull with what appeared to be narrow lasers or beams of plasma.

Morphus turned to them and said, "Be ready..." However, before either Tobin or Liberty could respond, the alien had kicked off the deck, and flung itself out into the hangar. The power of the vault shook some of the loose glass from the wall, and Liberty watched in astonishment as Morphus soared towards the Revocater. Then the alien entity transformed in mid-flight, reshaping its arms into wide, blade like appendages, and using them to glide gracefully towards its targets.

Before the drones had realized what was happening, Morphus had sliced through two of the spider-like machines like a flying sword. It then morphed the blade-like weapons back into arms, and landed, cat-like, on the hull of the Revocater. The remaining seed drones immediately reacted, halting their efforts to cut through the hull, and instead rounding on Morphus.

"Hey, Buffalo Bill, this is your cue!" said Liberty, thumping Tobin on the shoulder.

But Tobin just stared back at her, confused. "Buffalo who?"

"Just start shooting!" cried Liberty, throwing her tonfa-wielding hands into the air.

Tobin jolted into action, aiming the pistol out through the opening. "This is never going to work!" he said, as Morphus fought the first seed drone. The alien remained in human form, but seemed to shift and re-shape itself to dodge and deflect the javelin-like prongs of the seed drones.

Tobin fired, but instead of a bullet, the pistol released a narrow column of energy. It flew out towards the Revocater and slammed into its hull, a few meters behind the nearest seed drone.

"Shit!" Tobin swore, as two of the drones spun around and broke off from the group. They appeared to be scanning the walls and walkways, looking for whoever had fired the shot.

"Try again!" cried Liberty. "Just focus on the one you want to hit, and do as Morphus said. Trust yourself, like you did on Chrome One!"

The two seed drones stopped scanning, and their arrow-shaped body sections seemed to be aimed directly at where Liberty and Tobin were hiding. "Now would be a good time!" urged Liberty, as the drones started scurrying towards them.

Tobin took a deep breath, aimed and fired. A bolt soared out ahead, but this time it landed squarely in the center of an approaching drone, burning a deep trough into its black armor. The seed drone collapsed, its legs falling out from under it. However, the second had already moved beyond Tobin's firing arc, beneath the many levels of balconies that surrounded the hangar.

"Keep firing at the ones attacking Morphus!" shouted Liberty, stepping outside onto the wide walkway.

"Where are you going?" replied Tobin, firing again and taking out another seed drone that was trying to get behind Morphus.

"To get ready for the one you missed!" Liberty called out, spinning the strange alien tonfas into a ready position.

The view of the Revocater from the walkway was even more breathtaking, and she wondered how such a titanic vessel could possibly get into orbit. However, her attention was soon drawn to the continuing fight between Morphus and the drones. More of the machines had appeared now, scurrying along walkways at lower levels, before leaping onto the hull of the Revocater. Tobin fired again, and an energy bolt raced out, crippling the drone closest to Morphus.

"Keep it up!" Liberty called back, but then the scythe-like legs of a spider drone appeared over the barrier, and dug into the walkway. Liberty sucked in deep lungfuls of the cool air, and watched as the machine hauled itself onto the balcony, and twisted its arrow-like body to face her.

The machine advanced cautiously towards Liberty, but then stopped as another bolt of energy raced out from Tobin's pistol, destroying a drone on the Revocater. The seed drone instantly turned towards the opening, seeming to spot Tobin as he leant out and aimed again.

"Oh no you don't, you alien bastard," Liberty shouted, before she advanced towards the seed drone. If it wanted to get at Tobin, it would have to go through her first.

The spider-like machine had greater reach, and it attacked first, lashing out at Liberty with one of its legs. She reacted quickly and blocked the attack, half expecting the force of the strike to bowl her over. Remarkably, instead the tonfa repelled the drone's metal leg, as if it had rebounded off a rubber wall. Liberty glanced at the weapons in her hands in disbelief, noticing that they were now glowing, like her skin.

The drone attacked again, and Liberty blocked with the same result. However, this time she was alert enough to dart forward, and follow up with a counter-attack. Liberty swung one of the tonfas in an arc, attempting to strike the drone's central mass. The machine stepped back out of range, but instead of slashing empty air, a column of energy extended from the long end of the tonfa, and lashed across the drone's hull like a whip. The drone wavered on its spindly legs, and Liberty saw that there was a deep gash melted into its triangular body.

This time Liberty didn't stop to question the weapon's unusual capabilities. She attacked low, and swept the drone's legs from under it, sending the machine crashing to the deck. She then followed with a punch, and again a blast of energy accompanied the blow. The blast bored a neat circular hole all the way through the drone's body, even melting through the walkway below it.

Liberty stepped away from the smoldering mass, and again looked at her weapons in astonishment. Then she noticed that Tobin had stopped firing, and turned to check on him, her pulse racing higher. Tobin was leaning out of the opening, staring at Liberty with a look that was part amazement, part terror.

"That was insane!" Tobin shouted, as if he were watching some sort of extreme sport.

"Stop looking at me and keep shooting, damn it!" Liberty yelled back, observing that Morphus had just been knocked down. Three drones had surrounded it, and Liberty could see another three, working their way around the walkway towards them.

"Shit! We're going to have more visitors!" cried Liberty, rushing back inside the viewing gallery, as Tobin picked off one of the drones surrounding Morphus. Another two drones had landed on the Revocater, and had resumed cutting into the hull.

"Take out those ones," said Liberty, pointing to the new arrivals. "We can't let them get inside the Revocater. Morphus can handle the others." Tobin nodded, and took aim, while Liberty added, "At least, I hope it can..." However, it was said so quietly that Tobin didn't hear her.

Suddenly two drones smashed through the glass at the far end of the viewing gallery. Liberty took up position between the drones and Tobin, remembering Morphus' instruction to defend him. "I wonder what the range is on these things?" she mused to herself, as the drones clambered inside.

Liberty focused on the closest drone, which was still twenty meters away, and executed a double thrust towards it with the tonfas. Two bolts of energy shot from the ends of the weapons like arrows and bored into the drone's hull. Liberty smiled, but then another two machines clambered through the opening. Morphus' words about not being a hero came to mind. "We need to fall back," she called over to Tobin. "I can't take out all of them!"

Tobin fired again, destroying another drone, then swore. "Shit, one of them has started cutting into the hull, I have to get it first!"

"Make it fast!" Liberty called back, as the three seed drones inside the viewing gallery clustered together. They appeared more reticent about advancing on Liberty, after witnessing the brutal destruction of the first drone. However, as

Morphus had alluded to earlier, their actions denoted a more animalistic intelligence than a sentient one. They were like pack predators, cautiously weighing up whether they could take down a larger prey.

"Hurry!" Liberty urged again, as one of the drones finally began to advance. Liberty rushed out to meet it, swinging the tonfas at its base, before it was within striking distance. Again, a whip-like column of energy lashed out, swiping the machine's legs out from under it. It toppled to the floor and skidded towards Liberty, but before she could get out of its path, the drone thrust a metal limb at her, striking her in the chest.

"Got it!" Tobin shouted excitedly, but then he turned to see Liberty reeling backwards and falling flat on her back. He fired a snapshot at the drone, putting it down for good, but now the other two were also advancing fast. It was like they had tasted the scent of blood, and were moving in for the kill.

Tobin rushed towards Liberty and fired again, winging one of the drones, but still it came forward. He then hooked his hands underneath Liberty's arms and hauled her back towards the room that Morphus had opened for them. Liberty groaned, and half-heartedly punched a tonfa towards their attackers. Another arrow-like bolt shot out, taking out a leg of one of the drones, but it was not enough to destroy it, and merely delayed its relentless advance.

Tobin hauled Liberty over the threshold of the door and let her shoulders fall, before firing again. The bolt of energy struck the closest drone squarely in its center of mass, sending it down. Yet one still remained, and another had just entered at the far side of the gallery.

Liberty groaned and pushed herself upright as Tobin hit a panel on the wall, causing thick double doors to slam shut.

"I don't know how to lock it!" Tobin called out, throwing his arms wide in desperation.

Liberty shot up and slammed the end of the tonfa into the panel. She felt physically drained, and this time there was no blast of energy, but the panel still smashed. "Hopefully, that will hold them," she said, sliding her back down against the wall.

Tobin nodded, but then he noticed Liberty's new jacket, and let out a low whistle. "Wow, that was close..." he said, pointing to the alien fabric.

Liberty looked and saw a scar running across the alien material, where the drone had swiped it. The fibers had not split, and she figured that was the only reason she was still alive.

"We're not out of this yet," replied Liberty. "Morphus is still out there, and so are those things."

"Then I guess we have to hope Morphus wasn't exaggerating about its 'highly-advanced combat abilities'," said Tobin, resting back against the thick double doors. "At least we're safe in here."

No sooner had Tobin spoken the words than a dagger of plasma burst through the door, inches from his head. He threw himself away as the scalpel-like flame slowly began to cut through the metal.

"You had to say it, didn't you?" said Liberty, pushing herself up, and spinning the tonfas against her forearms. However, the glow of the alien metal, and of her hands, had faded almost to nothing. "I think these things draw some energy from our bodies," she said, feeling weaker than ever. She could barely hold the weapons up.

Tobin, similarly, looked pale and exhausted. "Well, it was certainly an adventure," he said, with a fatalistic air.

"Hey, we're not giving up yet," said Liberty. "Not before I get to fly that giant starship!"

The dagger of flame completed its perfectly circular path around the door, then vanished. They waited, breathless, holding their weapons tightly, as the chunk of metal was pushed inward. It slammed to the deck, sending vibrations rattling through Liberty's bones. Then the legs of the machine entered, before they slowly pulled through the arrow-like body of the seed drone.

Tobin fired, but the bolt was feeble compared to those he'd shot earlier, barely scorching the surface of the alien metal. Liberty roared and then charged forward, before striking the drone's center of mass, but it was like hitting an anvil with a hollow copper pipe. A sharp pain ran through her hand, and she stumbled back, dropping the tonfa to the floor. Tobin immediately rushed in to help her, but was then struck by one of the drone's flailing legs, and sent flying back into the room.

"Tobin!" cried Liberty, scrambling to his side. His augmented jacket had absorbed the brunt of the blow, but there was still a deep gash cut into his flesh, where he'd left it unbuttoned around his chest. "Damn your stupid Martian vanity," she said, but Tobin's eyes were shut, and he was limp in her arms.

Liberty heard the scrape of metal on metal, and turned to see the seed drone finish clambering through the opening. She gripped her remaining tonfa tightly and sprang up, but there was barely any strength left in her arms.

The drone raised one of its scythe-like legs, ready to strike, but then it suddenly froze. Liberty waited, heart thumping in her chest, as the drone then slid forwards and crumpled to the deck. There it lay still, a gaping hole punched through the rear of its body. Above it, standing in the opening, was Morphus.

Liberty threw down her weapon, and then again dropped to Tobin's side. "Morphus, help him, he's hurt."

Blood leaked from the gash in Tobin's chest, and Liberty tried to press on it to stem the flow, however, the warm, red liquid just oozed through her fingers. Morphus hurried inside and knelt calmly next to Tobin. The alien placed its hand on his chest, alongside Liberty's, and it began to glow and became amorphous, before flattening, like a sheet of metal foil. Morphus slid the glowing metal sheet underneath liberty's blood-soaked palms and formed a tight seal over the wound.

Liberty sat back, utterly exhausted. The exertion from the fight and the stress of Tobin's injury had taken almost everything out of her. Then she noticed that Morphus also appeared to be injured, and her pulse raced higher again. The alien was still in its female form, but parts of its body were featureless, as if Morphus was a sculpture that hadn't been fully finished.

"You're hurt too," said Liberty, moving to Morphus' side and examining the damage.

"I will be fine," said Morphus, smiling at Liberty. "The Revocater can repair my damaged systems, and now that the seed drones are destroyed, we are free to enter it."

Liberty nodded and looked down at Tobin again. He was unconscious, and his white jacket was soaked red, but Morphus had at least managed to stop the bleeding. "What about Tobin?" she asked, urgently. "Can you help him too?"

Morphus' smile disappeared, and its eyes became more solemn. It looked at Liberty, and said, "I am afraid that I do not know."

CHAPTER 29

Griff practically jumped out of the shuttle and onto the gravel surface of the lot in Swinsler's Shipyard. He'd never been more glad to get off a ship before in his life. It was early evening in San Francisco and the cool, fresh air was a welcome tonic. Griff sucked in several deep breaths and cleared his nose onto the dirt, in an attempt to rid his body of the shuttle's stench. Griff was used to the stale, recycled atmosphere of an RGF Patrol Craft, but the cockpit of the shuttle had reeked like a dirty fish tank. He breathed deeply a couple more times, then plucked a cigarette from his shirt pocket, placed it into his mouth and lit it.

"Those things will kill you," said Cutler, stepping out of the shuttle beside Griff. He had done a complete shut-down on the vessel, but there was still an ominous metallic tick coming from it, like a cooling kettle. "You do realize that they've been illegal on Earth for over a century?"

Griff sucked in the smoke and blew it out above his head, before scowling at the mercenary. "Your concern is touching, but how about you mind your own damn business?"

Cutler didn't react and instead looked towards the small complex of pre-fab office pods. These cheap, temporary structures constituted both Swinsler's place of work and his home residence. A door opened, and the yellow-haired figure of Swinsler waddled out towards them.

"I would suggest that..." Cutler began, but Griff cut him off, impatiently.

"Yeah, yeah, you do all the talking, I get it," Griff snapped. Now that he had a plan that didn't involve needing the mercenary, his tolerance for biting his tongue had all but vanished.

Cutler's eyes narrowed and his jaw tightened, but again he didn't react to Griff's insolence, at least not verbally. Griff watched him and gestured towards the ship dealer. "Well, get on with it then..." said Griff, rudely inviting Cutler to take the initiative, as he'd suggested.

"You can't park that thing there!" Swinsler's nasally voice shouted out to them. He was still more than ten meters away, but his round spectacles were in his hands, rather than on his similarly round face. Swinsler polished the lenses on the bottom of his lime green sweater, while adding, "This is a private lot; you'll have to move it!" Then he hooked the spectacles over his ears, finally bringing the face of Cutler Wendell into sharper focus. His aggravated expression and whiny aggressiveness instantly switched to simpering platitudes. "Oh, Mr. Wendell, I am so sorry, I had no idea it was you!" he blurted out, before shooting Cutler an oily smile.

Griff laughed at the ship dealer's transparently sycophantic response, before sucking in another lungful of smoke. Swinsler's eyes scrunched up as he looked at Griff for the first time, but he remained placid.

"And who is your new companion?" he asked, his eyes flitting between Cutler and Griff. "I do hope nothing untoward happened to the previous one? Tory wasn't it?"

Griff shook his head again. He knew people like Swinsler; while his job appeared on the surface to be trading starships, it was clear that the weaselly man's real trade was in information and secrets. He watched Cutler eagerly, wondering how much information he'd divulge, but the mercenary was as cagey as ever.

"Who he is, why I'm here, or any other similar question is none of your concern," replied Cutler, before tossing the shuttle's ID fob at him. The dealer juggled with the device, before finally managing to close his sweaty palm around it. "You know the drill."

"Yes, of course," replied Swinsler, again with an oily smile. "I trust that you require my special kind of accommodation?" Swinsler added, though the question seemed superfluous.

"Yes, the usual arrangement," replied Cutler.

Swinsler nodded, but then quickly adopted a more doubtful expression, "Excellent, although with all the heightened military activity at the moment, it will be more challenging – not to mention expensive – to ensure your secrecy."

"I'm sure you'll manage," said Cutler, dryly, as Griff laughed and shook his head again. He had to admire the slimy dealer's boldness, if nothing else. Then Cutler added, "The shuttle needs repairs. I'm sure you can make up your additional costs by over-charging me to fix it."

"Oh, I would never..." Swinsler began to protest, but Cutler was done talking, and just turned away and addressed Griff instead.

"There's a shelter underneath this lot where we can lay low for a while," he said, before gesturing for Griff to go ahead. "I'll show you the way."

Griff sucked in the last of the cigarette and flicked the stub to the ground. Cutler seemed to have intentionally mimicked Griff's curt gesture earlier, which made him suspicious. However, he was too tired to care. All he wanted was something soft to lie on, and a stiff drink. "This place had better be more comfortable than that piece-of-crap shuttle you lumbered us with," he grumbled, before walking towards the pre-fab that Cutler had indicated.

Swinsler then anxiously shuffled towards Griff, while calling out, "No, the entrance is..."

"I know where to go, Swinsler," Cutler cut-in sharply, and with uncharacteristic venom. He then glared back at the little man, who immediately halted his advance towards Griff, before shrinking away, apologetically.

Griff had seen such fierce intensity from Cutler perhaps only once before, when they were on the alien space station. At that time Cutler had lashed out at Griff, and demonstrated his clear contempt for him. The mercenary's similar reaction now only heightened Griff's feelings that he was planning something.

"Just get to work fixing the shuttle," Cutler demanded, still addressing Swinsler. "We may need to leave at a moment's notice."

Swinsler withdrew, bowing his head slightly. Griff felt his pulse quicken, but he continued on towards the pre-fab, his mind racing. *What was Swinsler about to say?* Griff asked himself. *'No, the entrance is...' not in there? Was that it? He's leading me to the wrong building, but why?* Then a chill ran down Griff's spine, as he suddenly realized that Cutler was preparing to make a move. He cursed himself for not having anticipated the mercenary's double-cross sooner, but now Cutler's choice of timing was obvious to him.

Cutler had already benefited from Griff's RGF credentials to get him to Earth, without being detected. Now, Griff was merely superfluous to requirements – he was excess baggage that Cutler intended to cut loose.

Griff knew he had to act quickly. Cutler would not want to cause a scene, and potentially draw unwanted attention to the lot. Griff guessed that this was why Cutler was leading him towards one of the pre-fabs. He assumed that as soon as Griff set foot inside the building, the mercenary would try to take him out. Griff had to stall him, and find a way to flip the situation to his advantage instead, otherwise he was dead.

"So, how did you find out about this place, anyway?" asked Griff, thinking on his feet and trying to find a way to delay Cutler. He glanced back at the mercenary, while reaching for his pack of cigarettes. He could see that Cutler's hand was already hovering near his holster.

"Word of mouth," replied Cutler, flatly. "Other mercenaries told me about it." Then he gestured to the building again, "Are you finished with your unnecessary questions now?"

Griff stopped and turned around, forcing himself to smile, and pretend to be Cutler's friend. The mercenary's impatience to get him inside the pre-fab only served to validate his suspicions. "These mercenaries; did they tell you about this place willingly or unwillingly?" Griff asked, as Cutler slowed, to avoid overtaking him.

"What does it matter?" replied Cutler, tartly. "Just get inside, we're wasting time."

Then Griff deliberately fumbled the pack of cigarettes, letting it fall onto the gravel surface in front of Cutler's feet. The mercenary stopped just short of stepping on the packet.

"Shit. You wouldn't mind grabbing that for me, would you?" said Griff, his heart now pounding like a drum. "It's my last packet, and I won't get another while we're on Earth."

Cutler sighed despairingly, and reached down for the cigarettes. "You would live longer if you just let me stamp on them instead," said Cutler, snatching the packet into his hand.

Griff took his chance and drew his weapon sharply, before aiming it at the top of Cutler's head, "No, I think I'll live longer without *you* around," he said, as Cutler froze, then glared up at him. "Do you think I'm stupid?" Griff spat, "I knew you only needed me to get back on Earth. And I knew you'd double-cross me as soon as we got there, just like you're trying to do now."

Cutler rose slowly, cigarette packet in hand. He looked at the pistol, and then into Griff's eyes. "Put the weapon down, Inspector," he said, appearing calm, but Griff could see the flicker of fear in his eyes. "I have no reason to kill you; we still need each other. We have more chance of evading the Council if we work together."

Griff laughed, "I won't need to evade the Council once I hand them your dead body, and pin the Devan girl's escape on you," he said. Griff felt suddenly invigorated. If he handed Cutler over to the Council, plus whatever credits he had left as a gesture to compensate for their losses, he was sure it would be enough to get the criminal gang off his back. Then the credits that Wash paid him for saving her scrawny ass would reimburse him several times over. It couldn't have worked out better if he'd planned it. "I'm afraid this is where our partnership ends," he sneered, repeating the words that Cutler had spoken to Tory, before the mercenary had abandoned her on Chrome One.

Then unexpectedly he heard Swinsler's voice shout out, "Who are you? What are you doing here?"

Griff scowled and shot a glance over to Swinsler, who was standing just outside the door of his office. Griff could see a figure approaching the dealer, but he couldn't quite make them out in the gloomy light. Suddenly his weapon was slapped from his hand, and Cutler rushed forward, driving Griff back and into the wall of the pre-fab building.

Griff yelped as his head slammed against the wall, then he saw Cutler reach for his own weapon. Survival instincts kicked in, and Griff grabbed the mercenary's wrist, forcing it down so that he couldn't get a shot. They wrestled, Griff trying to shake the pistol from Cutler's grasp, while the mercenary hammered him repeatedly against the wall, trying to break his hold. Despite Griff's greater height, Cutler was by far the stronger of the two men. He overpowered Griff and forced him to his knees before driving an elbow into his craggy face.

Griff collapsed to the gravel, blood pouring from his nose. His weapon lay on the ground a few meters away and, to his horror, the alien crystal fragment was sitting beside it. He patted down his jacket, pressing bloody hand prints to the fabric, and realized that the relic must have fallen out during the fight.

"I have always despised you, Inspector Griff," spat Cutler, aiming his weapon at Griff's head. He appeared not to have noticed the crystal on the ground to his side. "I despise your arrogance, your over-inflated opinion of your abilities, and your abject cowardice. I even despise your ridiculous mustache! You are and always were nothing without that RGF shield."

Griff wiped the blood from his nose and mouth, and spat bloody saliva onto the gravel by Cutler's feet. "So, what does that make you?" he hit back. If Cutler was going to kill him, he'd be damned if the jumped-up mercenary would get any satisfaction from him. "All you are is a hired hand. At least I was something. You? You'll always be someone else's errand-boy!"

Cutler tightened his grip on the pistol. His face was red with fury, and all traces of his trademark composure were gone. "At least I won't be your errand-boy any longer. Goodbye, Inspector."

Griff had nothing to lose. He dove for his weapon, but fell tantalizingly short of it. Despair overcame him, and he just lay, face down in the gravel, waiting for Cutler to end his life.

"Do it!" Griff growled, tasting the gravel in his mouth. Then he shut his eyes tightly, and yelled, "Do it, already!"

The crack of a pistol firing filled the air, but after the report had faded to nothing, Griff found that he was still alive. Tentatively, he lifted his head off the dirt and saw Cutler also lying on the ground close by. Griff frowned, and pushed himself to his knees, unable to make sense of what had happened. He stared down at the mercenary, who was groaning in agony while clutching his shoulder, before turning to look in the direction the shot had come from. Standing in the lot, with smoke oozing from the barrel of her weapon, was Jane Wash.

Griff scrambled to his feet, too stunned to speak, as Wash ran towards him. Then he spotted Cutler, scurrying away behind one of the pre-fabs, and he rushed to pick up his weapon. It was then that he noticed the crystal had gone. "Shit!" Griff cursed, punching the air in frustration.

"Get out of the damn way," Wash called out, causing Griff to spin around. She was waving her weapon at him, desperate for him to step aside. "Griff, move!"

Griff ducked down as Wash ran alongside him, aiming off towards where Cutler had last been seen. However, the mercenary had gone, leaving a thin trail of blood on the gravel.

"You idiot, you let him get away!" Wash cursed, before turning back to Griff. He was still too much in shock to react. "Well, don't just stand there, go and find him!" Wash yelled in his face.

The shrill shout of his former commander jolted his senses. It was like being back in the RGF briefing room again, while Wash dished out scoldings and orders. Suddenly alert, Griff grabbed his weapon off the gravel floor and followed the trail of blood, noting that Cutler's weapon still lay discarded. Wash moved around the other side, and together they pursued the trail until they reached the perimeter fence of the lot.

"Where the hell did he go?" shouted Griff, spinning around and checking the darker nooks and crannies of the lot. "He couldn't have climbed the fence, not with his arm all shot up like that."

Wash moved to the fence and tugged on the wire. A flap lifted up; it was just enough for a man to squeeze through.

"Damn it!" snarled Griff, peering through the fence to spot the mercenary. However, Swinsler's lot was alongside a maze of abandoned and part-derelict warehouses and industrial units. It would have been easy for Cutler to slip away unseen, and in the darkness, Griff knew they had no hope of finding him.

"I have only been here for five minutes, and already you've screwed this up!" snapped Wash, before kicking the fence.

Griff glared at Wash. It hadn't taken long for her contempt and condescension to surface. However, unlike Cutler Wendell, he actually needed his spiky former commanding officer to get out of the new mess he was in. "He's shot up and unarmed. He won't be a problem for us any time soon," said Griff, standing his ground. "And we'll be off this rock long before he is."

Wash glowered back at him and holstered her weapon. "You'd better be right," she snarled, jabbing a manicured finger at him. This time, however, her nail was chipped. She then turned on her heels, and set off back towards Swinsler's office. "At least you still have that alien crystal," she added, glancing back at him.

Griff winced and he could tell that Wash had immediately read his expression correctly. His former commander stopped, and spun back to face him.

"Are you telling me that you *don't* have it?" Wash screeched, throwing her hands up in despair.

"Cutler has the damn crystal, okay?" replied Griff, though he chose not to explain how or when the mercenary had acquired it. "Or he has a fragment of it, at least."

Wash then folded her arms, "What do you mean he only has a fragment of it? What happened to the rest?"

"Look, I'll explain how later," said Griff, trying to head off another dressing-down.

Wash shook her head again, "You just can't do anything right, can you?"

"We don't need the damn crystal," Griff hit back again. At this point, even Cutler's company would have been preferable, he thought to himself. "You have the credits, and I can get us IDs. We have a shuttle. So, what does it matter?"

"That crystal is the only bargaining chip we have with the CET and MP authorities," said Wash. "Sooner or later this mess with the alien ship will blow over. And if the CET or MP military catch up with us, that crystal is our negotiating power. It's our insurance." Then she held Griff's eyes and pointed her finger at him again. He recognized the look at once; Wash had made her decision, and there was no reasoning with her. "We are not leaving until we have it back."

Seemingly content that she'd made her point, Wash started to head back towards the cowering form of Swinsler. The crooked dealer had apparently been quietly observing the scene as it unfolded.

"Getting it back won't be easy," Griff called out. He knew it was pointless to argue with Wash, but he also wanted to make his points heard. "Cutler will just sell it the first chance he gets."

However, Wash didn't stop walking this time. Instead, she just glanced back to Griff and said, "For your sake, Inspector, you'd better hope you get it back, before that happens."

CHAPTER 30

Hudson stepped off the Orion and onto the deck of the hangar bay at Deimos Station. After taking a hit from a seed drone during their escape from Sapphire Alpha, he wanted to get the Orion checked over properly. Moreover, as a consequence of their many alien upgrades, they were also low on fuel. Like a big V8 muscle car, the Orion was powerful, but not exactly economical.

Hudson hadn't wanted to rely on the services in the Gale Basin, and Tory had agreed. Council-run spaceports were notorious for supplying low-grade fuels, sometimes causing ships to become stranded, or even blow an engine. Besides, Hudson had considered it wiser in general not to allow criminal organizations to work on one's ship.

Deimos Station was unusually quiet. Besides the Orion, the only other vessels that were docked were MP military ships, and a couple of private shuttles. There was also only a skeleton crew on deck.

"Where is everyone?" Hudson asked, stepping up to the deck chief.

The man shrugged lazily, "This gossip about a giant alien spaceship has them all spooked, I think," he said, while looking over the Orion's manifest. "Not that I blame them. The MP folk are all in the lower decks, in their outpost here, so the rest of the station is dead."

Hudson nodded. News of Goliath had spread, and it was no surprise that people would want to return to their homes, whether on Mars or elsewhere in the core system or portal worlds. "So, why are you still here?" Hudson asked the deck chief, curious as to why he'd stayed, despite knowing about the threat.

"Are you kidding? I get triple time covering for all those chicken-shits that bunked off," he said, smiling. Then he waved a thumb towards the MP ships in the hangar. "Besides, have you seen the firepower in here? And word has it that all the top dog MP cruisers are in orbit around Mars too. Hell, if anything big, bad and alien does come at us, I figure the safest place is right here."

Hudson turned to look at the rows of MP gunboats in the hangar. Ordinarily, he would have considered the deck chief's reasoning to be sound. However, the man was blissfully ignorant of what Goliath was capable of.

He turned back to the deck chief, and fixed him with a sober stare. "Take my advice, chief, and get out of here while you can," he said, wiping the could-care-less look off the man's face. "Trust me, if that alien ship does come here, all the firepower in the MP's armada won't make a dent in it."

Hudson left the man to ponder what he'd said, and stared back at the gunboats. Thousands of people crewed the military ships of both the CET and MP fleets. However, that number paled in comparison to the millions on the portal worlds, and the billions on the planets, moons and space stations of the solar system. All would perish if Goliath's rampage was left unchecked.

Despite the threat from Goliath, the military build-up around Earth had also enflamed tensions between the MP and the CET. Admiral Shelby and Commodore Trent may have agreed to amass their fleets as a precautionary measure, but the deep mistrust between them remained.

Hudson had experienced the paranoia and intransigence of Admiral Shelby several times before. He could well imagine that the stuck-up MP commander would be more concerned about a CET invasion, than an attack from an alien mega-ship. Hudson shook his head. Despite their advances, and despite all the might of humankind's powerful military warships, it fell to him and a few others to save humanity. Because if they didn't stop Goliath then no-one would.

While Hudson was lost in his own thoughts, Tory had paid the docking fee and fuel costs, without being asked, and was now waiting for him by the docking bay exit.

"Given the lack of deck crew, it will be a few hours before the inspection is complete," said Tory. "Though it will be interesting to see what they make of the tech your friend Morphus added."

Hudson nodded, "Let them be confused," he replied, "so long as they tell me the Orion can still handle a few high-g burns, I don't care what they think. We've got a long way to travel yet."

"Well, I guess there's only one thing for it then," said Tory, walking through the archway and into the corridor outside.

Hudson raised a curious eyebrow, and followed her. "What's that then?"

Tory glanced back at him, and returned a matching eyebrow-raise. "We go for a drink, of course." Then she shrugged, casually, "Well, a few drinks, actually..."

Hudson smiled and jogged briefly to catch up with her. "I'm game, so long as you don't mind being the one to fly us down to Mars later," he said, remembering how the only person he'd ever seen put away more whiskey than Tory in one sitting was Ma. Then he remembered the miraculous pills that Ma had slipped him in the Landing Strip, before his raid on the UEC vault, and huffed a laugh. "Though if you happen to be stashing any nanolivers in one of those pouches on your belt, I guess we could have a proper session."

Tory glanced over at him, the faintest suggestion of a smile curling the corner of her mouth. She then popped open one of the pouches on her belt, and removed a box. She shook it, and it rattled.

Hudson shook his head in astonishment, "You do have some, don't you?" he asked, but Tory just shrugged again, before slipping the box back into the pouch and refastening the popper.

"Top mercenary tip; drink hard, but always stay sober," she answered. "That way your enemies will always think you're vulnerable."

"You're pretty incredible, Tory Bellona," said Hudson. "Has anyone ever told you that?"

They reached the door of The Winchester, and Tory pushed it open. "I've been called a lot of things, but never that."

"Well, there's a first time for everything," said Hudson, stepping through the door. "Let's drink to many more first times."

"Like the first time stopping an alien invasion from wiping out the human race?" said Tory, as she moved in beside Hudson. The door slammed shut behind them, as if to reinforce the weight of Tory's question.

Hudson sighed and rubbed the back of his neck, wearily. "Well, when you put it like that, I think I definitely need a few drinks."

Tory stepped further into the bar, but then stopped and pressed her hands to her hips. "I think we might be serving ourselves."

Hudson hadn't even noticed until then that the bar was completely deserted. He walked up to the counter, but Roy the barman wasn't there; not even hiding under his bucket. Hudson reached over the counter top and grabbed a couple of glasses, while Tory suddenly vaulted the bar like a gymnast. He watched her with interest as she sauntered along the row of antique weapons hung on the rear wall, before stopping in front of one in particular. Hudson smiled knowingly, finally understanding what the mercenary was up to.

Tory delicately lifted the Winchester rifle from its mounting brackets on the wall, and began examining it with a sort of loving deference. Then she noticed that Hudson was staring at her, with an accusatory look on his face.

"What?" she said, scowling back at him.

Hudson held up his hands, "I'm not judging, but isn't that technically stealing?"

Tory appeared to be unmoved by Hudson's indictment. She gently rested the rifle on the bar, and grabbed a bottle of the strongest bourbon she could find. Placing it alongside the glasses that Hudson had retrieved, she met his eyes again, and said, "Shut up and pour."

Hudson shrugged. There no point arguing with Tory, especially when she was armed with two lethal weapons. He popped open the bottle and poured two large measures.

"Technically, that's stealing too," said Tory, having a little dig of her own.

"I was going to leave some hardbucks behind the counter," lied Hudson, but Tory was having none of it.

"We both know that the few hardbucks you have left are tucked inside Liberty's jacket," she said, picking up her glass. Then she tapped the Winchester with her other hand, and added, "Besides, Buckethead won't miss this. And, where we're going, we'll need the extra firepower."

Hudson couldn't argue with Tory's final point. He picked up his glass, chinked it against Tory's, and they both drained the contents in one. "Do you even have any bullets for that thing?" said Hudson, as Tory re-filled the glasses.

Tory whipped her Colt Frontier Six-Shooter revolver out of her holster. Hudson had terrifying flash-backs to earlier, more hostile moments in their relationship, and almost threw up his hands in surrender.

"This is the Model 1873 Winchester rifle," she said, tapping it with the barrel of her revolver, "which, helpfully, uses the same ammunition as this six-shooter." She holstered the revolver again, then tapped one of her many other belt pouches with the tip of her finger. "As for ammunition, that's what all these are for. Most of them, anyway."

Hudson picked up his glass, "Right now, this is the only round I'm interested in," he said, taking another mouthful.

The door then suddenly flung open and a man bustled inside. Tory instinctively drew her revolver and aimed it, clicking back the hammer. The man froze, and Hudson let out a huge breath of relief, realizing who it was.

"What are you two doing in here?" said Roy the barman. He then noticed the revolver aimed at him and thrust his hands towards the ceiling.

Tory de-cocked the six-shooter, and holstered it again, before answering, "We're having a drink. What does it look like?"

Roy frowned, but seemed to accept Tory's statement of the obvious, and continued to bustle towards them. "Well, you'll have to finish, because I'm locking up and getting off this station," he said, moving behind the bar. He grabbed a fresh garbage bag, and started to go through the drawers and cupboards, tossing various items into the bag. "Everyone has gone, apart from the MP, and they never come in here, anyway. Stuck up assholes..." he grumbled, before moving to the till and opening it with his thumbprint. He tossed whatever hardbucks were inside into the bag, then bustled past Tory again, before spotting the antique lever-action rifle on the counter. "What are you doing with that?" he asked, nervously. He was careful to stay out of her striking range, and ensure that the question didn't sound like an accusation. Hudson smiled; he'd almost forgotten about Tory's fierce reputation.

Tory rested on the bar, and twisted her body to face Roy, before taking a sip of bourbon. "I'm going to shoot some Council thugs with it on Mars," she said, with all the casual menace that used to both terrify and enthrall Hudson. "Do you have a problem with that?"

The barman shook his head vigorously, "No, no, just asking! Feel free to borrow it." Hudson was impressed at his casual slipping-in of the word 'borrow'. It was a cunning and non-aggressive method of inferring that Tory should return it.

"Sure, I'll bring it back," said Tory. "Assuming we don't all get vaporized by this planet-killing alien ship, of course." Roy's eyes widened and he almost dropped his now full garbage bag. Tory took another sip of bourbon, before adding, "Weren't you about to leave?"

"Yes, and you should too," said Roy, grabbing an epaper from a shelf under the counter, before sliding it in front of Hudson. He then hustled back around the bar and made a bee-line for the door. Hudson saw Tory duck underneath the counter to grab something, before she called out to Roy.

"Hey, you might be needing this," Tory yelled at the barman. She then tossed the bucket that Roy used to place on his head during bar fights towards him. It clattered across the floor, and spun to a stop by his feet.

"Keep it!" Roy called back. He pushed through the door and was gone.

Hudson turned back to Tory, and shot her another reproving look.

"What? I have a reputation to uphold," shrugged Tory, before finishing her bourbon, and topping it up.

Hudson laughed, and finished his drink. Placing the glass back down on the counter, his attention was then drawn to the epaper that Roy had slid towards him. He picked it up, and swiped to the lead story in the news section, his brow furrowing more deeply the more he read.

"What is it?" asked Tory, leaning closer with her elbows on the bar.

"Goliath," said Hudson, ominously. "Sapphire Alpha was just the start. It's taken out Emerald One, Medusa Four, Ruby Prime and Cerberus One too," he continued, scanning ahead. "And those seed ships have been spotted attacking many of the smaller colonies on the other OPW worlds too."

Tory frowned, "Ruby Prime is where union headquarters was based. If that planet has been destroyed, then the OPW is finished."

Hudson nodded, "And if we don't stop it then Earth will be next. We'd better get going."

"Wait," said Tory, re-filling Hudson's glass. "There's one piece of good news in that bulletin that we should drink to."

"Really?" replied Hudson, wondering how the annihilation of entire planets, and the end of the Union of Outer Portal Worlds, could be something worthy of a toast.

"If Cerberus One is gone then so is New Providence," Tory said, raising her glass. "That will weaken the Council and send them into a panic. It might make what we have to do next a bit easier."

Hudson sighed, "That's pretty thin as far as silver linings go, but I guess every little helps." Then he raised his glass, and said, "To silver linings."

"And to the next adventure," Tory replied, before they both knocked back their drinks.

Hudson slid off his stool and felt his legs wobble. He had to grab the counter again to steady himself. "I think I'll be needing one of those nanolivers soon enough," he said, before finally getting control of his limbs.

Tory vaulted the bar again, and landed like a cat on the other side. "I already took one before we left the Orion," she said, smiling.

Hudson shook his head, "Drink hard, but stay sober, right? I have to learn that one."

"We have time," said Tory, grabbing the bottle of bourbon and handing it to Hudson. "I'm not going anywhere." Tory then picked up the Winchester rifle, before hooking her arm through

Hudson's. "Come on, let's go. With any luck, we can make the Gale Basin by morning, Martian time," she said.

Hudson accepted Tory's help, though in truth he didn't really need it. He was as much tired as he was drunk, but it felt good to have her close. "Okay, but you're driving," he said, and Tory laughed. It wasn't much, little more than a muted chuckle really; but it was good to hear.

Hudson Powell and Tory Bellona pushed through the doors of the Winchester, and entered the deserted corridor of Deimos Station. Then, arm-in-arm, they set off back to the Orion, and back into the fight.

He should have felt afraid, but he didn't. It could have been the bourbon talking, he admitted, but with Tory at his side, and Liberty joining forces with Morphus, he truly felt like they had a chance. The Union of Outer Portal Worlds may have fallen, but they weren't finished yet. Not by a long shot. Not while he was still standing. And, most of all, not while one last Revocater still remained.

The end.

EPILOGUE

Goliath watched as another planet harboring the last offspring of the Corporeal race crumbled beneath its might. Its task was arduous, but gratifying. Soon it would have cleansed all of these other worlds of the corporeal stain, and be free to make its way to System 5118208 in order to complete its task.

However, the satisfaction it experienced at the obliteration of its latest target had been tainted. It still felt a niggling doubt that not all the Revocaters had been destroyed. It had been an age since Goliath had felt the presence of the guardian ships the Corporeals had designed to stop it. And because of this, it did not trust that its senses were accurate. Yet it also knew that one Revocater may have survived – the one that had banished it. The one that had defeated it.

The mere thought of that Revocater filled Goliath with rage. It hated the ship almost as much as the corporeals who had created it. However, if this last Revocater had endured, it would soon die alongside the beings it sought to protect. In some ways, Goliath hoped it had survived, because it would offer the great ship a chance at vengeance.

A portal flashed open and a seed drone emerged, before accelerating towards Goliath. The great ship hungrily assimilated the data from the vessel's sensors, eager to learn any news of the Revocater, but the Telescope had refused to co-operate, and lend Goliath its eye. This angered the great ship even further. It had been a mistake to spare it, Goliath realized. After it had finished its task, it would return to the homeworld and destroy the Telescope too. This time, nothing would remain of the Corporeal race, but rubble and twisted metal. This time, Goliath's own hubris would not stand in the way of its task.

Goliath assimilated the last of the data from the seed drone, learning that the Corporeal's planet had been reclaimed by nature. This pleased the great ship – it was as it should be – but then it found an anomaly. Some of the seed drones were unaccounted for.

Goliath assessed the information in more detail, scanning the location on the planet's surface where the drones had gone missing. A memory stirred, deep in the great ship's archives. It was a memory of before it had laid waste to the Corporeal's planet, and destroyed its many natural and artificial satellites and space stations. It delved deeper, seeing the planet's location in all the frequencies open to it. And then the image of what it was searching for suddenly resolved. Deep beneath the surface, hidden and buried for millennia, there was another Revocater.

Rage swelled inside Goliath, not only because the Revocater existed, but because it had missed the vessel during its initial assault on the homeworld. Goliath's failures shamed it, but it would not fail again. The fragments of corporeal life on the worlds beyond System 5118208 could wait, it decided. It would no longer delay the destruction of the only system it had originally failed to wipe clean. Then, and only then, it would turn its attention to the last Revocater. First, it wanted to the Revocater to witness its failure, as Goliath had once witnessed its own.

The great ship reprogrammed the seed drone and spat it back out into space. It would return to the homeworld and flush this last guardian ship out of its hole.

Goliath turned away from the fragmented remains of the planet, and began the next phase of its journey. Its consciousness was filled with thoughts of the last Revocater. This guardian ship would know failure, as Goliath had known it. Revocaters only existed to protect corporeal life;

it was their sole purpose. So its defeat would be even more crushing than Goliath's had been.

Goliath would cripple this last Revocater, and force it to witness the end of its purpose. It would know a dishonor greater than any living being in the galaxy. Then, Goliath would have had its revenge. Then, and only then, could the great ship finally rest.

TO BE CONTINUED

The Star Scavenger Series concludes in book five, The Last Revocater.

The Last Revocater:

READ THE OTHER BOOKS IN THE SERIES:

- Guardian Outcast
- Orion Rises
- Goliath Emerges
- Union's End
- The Last Revocater

ALSO BY THIS AUTHOR

If you enjoyed this book, please consider reading The Contingency War Series, also by G J Ogden, available from Amazon and free to read for Kindle Unlimited subscribers. Also available as an audiobook on Amazon, Audible and iTunes.

- The Contingency
- The Waystation Gambit
- Rise of Nimrod Fleet
- Earth's Last War

"Highly recommended - sci-fi fans will not be disappointed with this novel."
Readers' Favorite, 5-star review.

No-one comes in peace. Every being in the galaxy wants something, and is willing to take it by force...

ABOUT THE AUTHOR

At school I was asked to write down the jobs I wanted to do as a 'grown up'. Number one was astronaut and number two was a PC games journalist. I only managed to achieve one of those goals (I'll let you guess which), but these two very different career options still neatly sum up my lifelong interests in science, space and the unknown.

School also steered me in the direction of a science-focused education over literature and writing, which influenced my decision to study physics at Manchester University. What this degree taught me is that I didn't like studying physics and instead enjoyed writing, which is why you're reading this book! The lesson? School can't tell you who you are.

When not writing, I enjoy spending time with my family, walking in the British countryside, and indulging in as much Sci-Fi as possible.

You can connect with me here:
https://twitter.com/GJ_Ogden
https://www.ogdenmedia.net

Subscribe to my newsletter:
http://subscribe.ogdenmedia.net

Printed in Great Britain
by Amazon